A KISS BEFORE TROUBLE...

Evan needed no further encouragement. He took hold of her cheek and tilted her head back slightly before lowering his lips to hers. This time their embrace lasted even longer. Evan's tongue caressed Jessie's as his free hand roamed over her back. Slowly his mouth moved from hers and he covered her soft cheek with baby kisses. "I've wanted to do this to you ever since I laid eyes on you."

"Is that all you've wanted to do, Evan?"

"I can't even mention the rest..."

WESLEY ELLIS

LONE STAR

AND THE
DEADLY STRANGER

JOVE BOOKS, NEW YORK

LONE STAR AND THE DEADLY STRANGER

A Jove Book/published by arrangement with
the author

PRINTING HISTORY
Jove edition / July 1988

ISBN: 0-515-09648-2

Jove books are published by The Berkley Publishing Group,
200 Madison Avenue, New York, New York 10016.
The name "JOVE" and the "J" logo
are trademarks belonging to Jove Publications, Inc.

10 9 8 7 6 5 4 3 2 1

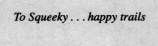

To Squeeky . . . happy trails

Chapter 1

The pair of riders reined in at the top of a grassy knoll. The broad expanse of prairie stretched out below them. In the faint light of a false dawn the sky was just barely distinguishable from the land, but to the south a grove of cottonwoods punctuated the flat horizon. With a pair of field glasses one could pick out the ranch house that stood among the trees. But these two travelers didn't need any help picking out the buildings of the Circle Star ranch; the Texas ranch was their home, and they knew every tree, every gully, every stone.

Jessica Starbuck, a tall, shapely woman with flowing blond hair studied the panorama with cool green eyes. A slow smile stretched across her pretty face. "That first sight always gives me a tingle."

"We haven't been home for a while," her companion answered. He was a lean, muscular man, with long, black hair, and a thin, dark mustache. He sat tall in the saddle, and stood close to six feet. In fact his height often confused people. His sallow complexion, though tanned from exposure to the elements, was clearly Oriental; but his stature was a product of his American father. Though born and bred in Japan, Ki had spent his adult years in America serving as a bodyguard, teacher, and friend to the woman he now rode beside.

Jessie shook her head. "Even if I'm gone only a day, when I get up on this rise I feel my pulse quicken."

Ki nodded. "Perhaps that's because your roots are here."

"You mean my heart doesn't skip a beat just because this is the most beautiful spot on all the earth?" she asked teasingly.

"Seeing as how the Circle Star is the heart of the Starbuck empire, it doesn't surprise me that you feel that way."

"Ki," she said sharply, "it has nothing to do with that. You know quite well that I'd give up all my other holdings sooner than lose the Circle Star." Her anger abated quickly, and her tone softened. "I can't think of a more ideal place, can you?"

A smile formed on Ki's smooth, handsome face. "Not for someone with ranching in her blood."

"I'll take that as a compliment," she said seriously, "mostly because I don't feel like dickering way out here. . . ."

"When you could be relaxing in paradise, down there," Ki finished for her.

Jessie couldn't help but smile. "I'll see you over a plate of flapjacks," she said gaily, then kneed her horse into a gallop.

It was a quiet time for the Circle Star. The hectic days of spring roundup had finished weeks ago. The cattle were sorted, the new calves were branded, and a large trail herd was already on its way to summer pasture. The hands who

2

stayed behind were busy with riding checks on the numer-
ous windmills that dotted the ranch. If the land wasn't
properly irrigated, the arid months of summer would
scorch the earth and kill the grass. It was essential that the
windmills were functioning properly. Often they required
nothing more than a good greasing, but there was a lot of
land to be covered and the men that went out were always
gone the better part of two weeks.

As lazy as the season seemed there was still plenty of
work to keep Jessie occupied. Correspondence had piled
high on her desk. She sat behind her father's large rolltop
desk, looking chagrined by the volume of letters that
needed to be answered. She had been at it all morning and
had hardly made a dent in the pile.

Ki entered, sat down in a leather chair, and offered a
sympathetic word. "Looks like homecoming isn't such a
bed of roses."

"What makes you say that?" Jessie said with a touch of
sarcasm.

Ki shrugged.

Jessie laughed. "It's just that I keep forgetting what the
first day back is like."

"It's one of the evil necessities of doing business. Your
father never liked it much, either."

Jessie showed interest at the mention of her father,
Alex, the founder of the Starbuck empire. "He seemed
much better suited to all this. . . ."

Ki laughed. "He used to sit in that chair and stare wist-
fully out the window. He had the same expression on his
face that you have now," he added with a smile.

"But he managed to keep everything running."

"So do you, Jessie."

"Yes, but I feel so swamped by all this."

"Don't forget, Jessie, in these past few years you've
managed to add considerably to the business. Starbuck En-

terprises are not only thriving; they've almost doubled."

"A lot of that has to do with my father. The seeds he planted years ago are now just coming into their own."

"I'm not arguing that, Jessie. Alex always did plan for the future. But I wouldn't underestimate your own achievements." Ki started to rattle off recent acquisitions. They included a meat-packing house, a silver mine, a shipping company, a controlling interest in a California bank, and a few hundred acres of northern grazing land. He was still going though the list when Jessie cut him short.

"You've made your point, Ki," she said with a smile.

"Good."

"Perhaps you've made it too well."

"I don't follow," Ki said with concern.

"Maybe I'm overstepping my limits. What do I know about banking?"

Ki started to smile, but changed his expression quickly when he realized Jessie was serious. "There are few people as capable as you," he said with equal seriousness.

"But when I come home and face this mountain of paperwork I think maybe I'm biting off more than I can chew. What *do* I know about banking, or for that matter, meat packing?"

"You know people," Ki said firmly. "You know who is honest. You can tell who is capable and hard working. And that talent is much more valuable than any tidbit of information you might learn about any specific business."

Jessie didn't look satisfied. "I think I'd like to be spending more time on the Circle Star. Just simply ranching." She gestured to the letters on her desk. "I'd be perfectly happy to sell all this off and settle down with a few thousand head of longhorns."

"But would that make others happy?"

"What do you mean, Ki? Who would care if I got out of the banking business?"

4

"I think there would be a lot of folks that would care," Ki answered.

Jessie's expression was an unspoken "Who?"

"Folks we don't know personally," Ki continued. "But just the same they're folks who need a safe place to put their money, or a bank that would give them a loan that they wouldn't have to break their backs repaying. There are plenty of hard-working folks who need a bank that can understand their special problems."

"Ki, my bank doesn't give money away."

"No, but the manager you hired understands that if a homesteader has one bad season he deserves another chance. Do you think the big Eastern banks give a farmer a second chance? Do you think they'll bankroll a wild-mustanger just because he's a hard worker?"

"You've made your point again," Jessie said with a sigh.

Ki shook his head. "Not completely. Alex didn't invest only to make money. He invested to give somebody he believed in a chance—a chance at doing something good, something that would benefit others. You're no different. We spend so much time away from the Circle Star because there are a lot of folks out there who need help. Folks who you willingly choose to help."

Jessie started to smile. "I reckon so. But still—"

"Any time you want to give up that responsibility—"

"You know that's out of the question," she shot back quickly. Then her tone softened. "It's a beautiful day. The sun is shining, the clouds are fluffy-white against a blue sky, and I can smell the grass." She stood up suddenly. "I'm going to take Sun out for a ride. We could both use it."

She caught sight of Ki smiling. "What's so amusing about taking my favorite horse out for a run?"

"For a moment there you sounded just like Alex."

5

"How so?"

"He would also get restless if he spent too much time at his desk."

"What was his solution?" Jessie wondered aloud.

Ki smiled. "If it were a nice day, he'd round up his little girl and go out for a ride."

A dusty, grimy man lay belly down in the tall grass. He lowered the field glasses, then, through cracked, stained teeth, spat out a long stream of dark tobacco juice. There was no mistaking the blond woman that just rode out of the barn. He had never laid eyes on her before, but there was no question as to her identity. She was Alex Starbuck's little girl. *Grown up to quite a gal,* he thought to himself. Then his smile grew even wider. This was going to be better than he ever imagined.

Chapter 2

The sun was hanging low in the sky when Jessie returned to the barn. A young stable hand rushed over to unsaddle her mount and rub the horse down.

"Afternoon, Miss Jessie," he said, without offering to help her dismount. He was not being rude or impolite; he would no sooner think of assisting her than he would Ed Wright, the ranch foreman. When he first started working on the Circle Star he had made the mistake of assuming Jessie rode like any other woman. He wouldn't make that mistake again.

"Fella came by with a message for you," he continued as he took hold of the animal's bridle.

"Is he in the cookhouse?" Jessie asked. It was common range hospitality to fix a messenger up with some food and a cup of hot coffee. Therefore Jessie was surprised when the young man shook his head.

"I did offer him some grub," he said quickly, "but he said he couldn't be stickin' around."

It was unusual for a rider, especially in the lazy days of summer, to pass up such an invitation, but there were times when a man was pressed for time, and Jessie didn't think anything of it. "Well, what did he have to say?" she asked.

"Said he just came from riding herd with the Double M—"

Jessie seemed to recall a spread by that name. "Up by the Canadian?" she wondered out loud.

Johnny nodded enthusiastically, impressed with his boss's knowledge. "Yup. He said it was a few miles north of the river."

"He have anything else to say?" Jessie prodded gently.

"Sorry, ma'am," the boy said self-consciously. "Said I should tell you that the Mora Creek done dried up."

"The Mora?" Jessie repeated to herself.

"I think it runs east-west through the badlands of the—"

"I know the Mora," Jessie snapped.

"Sorry, ma'am. I didn't mean to offend."

Jessie smiled. "No need to apologize, Johnny. Have you seen Ki?"

"'Bout an hour ago he was out shooting his bow."

Jessie walked quickly to the large oak that stood behind the main house. There she found Ki with his six-foot lacquered bow.

"I thought I'd spend a few hours relaxing," he started to say. Then he changed his tone when he caught sight of Jessie's expression. "What's wrong?"

"The Mora's gone dry."

Ki thought for a moment. "Ed's driving the herd in that direction." Jessie nodded and Ki continued. "That's one of the watering stops for the trail herd."

Jessie nodded again.

"One of the important ones," Ki added.

"And what's worse, if the Mora is dry, some of the other, smaller watering holes might also be dry."

Ki agreed. "It will make for a hard drive. We should try and get word to Ed. When did he leave?" he asked suddenly.

"Not more than a week ago."

"A fast rider should be able to catch him in a few days," Ki said.

"Who do you suggest I send, Ki?" A trace of a smile made her eyes sparkle. "Johnny doesn't know the trail that well, and the other hands are busy with their own chores."

"I'm available," Ki said matter-of-factly.

"Good. We can leave today and get a few miles in by sundown."

"We?" Ki asked with a grin. "What about all that paperwork sitting on your desk?"

Jessie smiled. "It'll hold." Then she turned serious. "It'll hold a lot better than those cattle trying to make it across the dry prairie."

Twenty minutes later Jessie and Ki were back on the trail, leading an extra pair of horses. The change of mounts would allow them to make quicker time. It was important to catch the trail herd as soon as possible. The Mora Creek was the only fresh water in a long strip of dry land. The herd would rely on that watering-stop. If Jessie couldn't catch the herd in time many head would die of thirst.

Ki and Jessie both understood that, and they rode at a good clip. They didn't worry about pacing their horses. In a few hours they would make camp for the night, and the animals would get their chance to rest then.

As for the two riders, they would catch what rest they could, but they wouldn't sleep well until they had caught up with the herd.

The next day passed uneventfully. Again they pushed on as long as the light held, making camp by the light of the

9

bright moon. They had just finished their meal when a change in the wind brought the distinct smell of burning mesquite.

"A cook-fire, not more than a mile from here," Ki noted.

"Another drive?" Jessie wondered at first. Then she changed her mind and shook her head. "We would have seen their dust."

"Riders coming from the north?" Ki suggested.

"Perhaps. Maybe they can tell us something more about the Mora."

"If they ran into our herd, perhaps they've even told Ed."

"That would certainly make things easier," Jessie said.

"There's only one way to find out," Ki said simply. But he, too, was hoping for the best.

"Guess we'll pay a neighborly call come sunup."

The sky was brightening but the sun had not yet risen when Jessie and Ki saw the three wagons grouped in a circle. There were two light wagons—small, maneuverable versions of the famous Conestoga covered wagon—and a simple buckboard. The wagons were not an unusual sight, but the lack of activity around them was. There was no sign of life, but even more surprisingly there were no signs of any animals, either. Not a horse nor an ox-team was anywhere to be seen.

"What do you think, Ki?" Jessie asked.

"This is where the smoke came from." He pointed to the distant pile of fresh ashes that was situated between the wagons. "Where the people are who built that fire remains to be seen."

"Let's go have a look," Jessie said and eased her horse forward.

"I'd be careful, Jessie," Ki started to say. But his warning was unnecessary.

10

Jessie had moved only a few yards closer when the crack of the rifle rang out. She had been shot at many times before, and had a sense about these things. How she could be certain could not be explained, but just the same she was positive that she was in no real danger. The shot was not meant to maim or kill her; it was meant as a warning. She remained in the saddle, though she did bring the horse up short.

Ki moved his horse next to her. "That answer any of your questions?"

"Does it answer yours?" she shot back with a smile. "It only makes me a sight more curious."

"You know what they say about curiosity, Jessie." Ki was talking casually, but he was anything but. His eyes scanned the seemingly deserted wagons, and his hand slowly pulled out a silver *shuriken* from his vest pocket.

"The wagon on the left, under the driver's seat," he said quickly.

Jessie nodded. She too saw the rifle barrel that was poking out at them. "Looks like that's the only one."

Ki nodded. "But it only takes one."

Despite Ki's added warning Jessie was still not too concerned, and she knew Ki shared her feelings. If he felt there was any danger, he would never allow her to stand exposed and in the open.

"Howdy, friend," she called out loudly. She heard some stirring in the wagon. Obviously the rifleman was not alone. "We were just passing through and—"

Jessie was cut off short by a woman's voice, which emanated from inside the wagon. "You fool, can't you see she's a woman?"

Jessie smiled to herself and eased her horse forward. But to be on the safe side she kept her hands up where they could been seen, and continued her friendly conversation. "My name's Jessica Starbuck, and this is Ki."

11

The man with the gun hopped down from the wagon. He was tall and broad-shouldered, with a thick head of wavy blond hair and wide-set, friendly blue eyes. Save for the Winchester in his hand, Jessie found everything about the man quite attractive.

She didn't have much time to ponder his looks before a shapely young woman stepped down next to him. There was no doubt the woman was beautiful. With her long, dark brown hair piled high on her head, her round, dark eyes, delicate nose, and soft, red lips, there was no question the woman was many a man's dream. But there was something incongruous about the pair. The man wore faded overalls and a plain muslin shirt, but the woman had on a long blue dress trimmed in lace. It was pinned in tight around the waist and accentuated her rounded hips and her large, full bosom. The man looked perfectly in place riding around the prairie, but the woman looked better suited to a San Francisco drawing-room. Jessie then noticed the heavy rouge on the woman's cheeks, and her dark blue eye-liner. For a quick moment Jessie flashed on just the sort of house a woman like that would be most at home in, but then quickly put the thought out of her mind.

"Forgive me, ma'am," the man started. "We weren't expecting any visitors."

"Were you expecting trouble?" Jessie countered.

"We've seen more than our share," the woman said bitterly.

"What she means is we didn't mean to be unfriendly; we just have to be a mite cautious."

Out of the corner of her eye, Jessie saw movement in the other covered wagon. She stiffened as the canvas flap drew back. Then she relaxed as three men climbed down.

"Didn't mean to startle you, ma'am" the first man said as he tipped his black bowler hat. He was a well-groomed, rather dapper man in his early thirties. His mustache was waxed, and his white shirt and striped silk vest looked clean and crisp. He definitely had an air of refinement about him, but Jessie could detect a shrewd, calculating mind behind the dark, shifty eyes.

"I reckon we might as well introduce ourselves," the man who held the Winchester said quickly. "My name's Evan. Evan Strummer.

Jessie slid down from her horse. "Pleased to meet you, Evan."

Ki followed Jessie's lead and dismounted too.

"And this is Miss Yvette DeVeau," Evan continued. The woman next to him did a short curtsy, staring at Ki all the while.

Evan continued. "And that's Warren . . ."

The dapper gentleman finished his own introduction. "Warren Blain Smith, at your service. And please call me Blain." He flashed a smile. "Everyone does."

The man next to him stepped forward somewhat nervously. "Jim Richards, ma'am." Though he had a soft, babylike face, Richards was somewhere in his mid twenties, and he didn't seem as innocent and naive as his looks implied. He was dressed in riding clothes, but he didn't wear them well. Jessie pegged him for a town merchant, one who knew enough to dress properly for wagon travel, but didn't yet have the experience to wear them comfortably.

The last man was Richard's complete opposite. He was an experienced ranch hand. Jessie could tell at once. It was not only in the way he wore his clothes, but in the way he stood and moved. There was something in his stance that said he would rather be on horseback than on his own two feet. He was broad-shouldered and solidly built, with a face that was tanned leather, and hands that were scarred and powerful. He was alert, if not somewhat tense, but his eyes seemed tired and bored. Jessie noted they were eyes that viewed his other companions with a good deal of scorn

13

and contempt. "The name's Buck," he said simply, making it clear he had no interest in saying any more.

Jessie turned back to Evan. "You were saying about trouble?"

"We've had more than our share," he repeated.

Jessie took a quick look around. "What happened to your animals?"

"Bandits," Evan answered simply.

Jim Richards elaborated. "Mexican *bandidos*," he shot out angrily. "Six of them. They took our food, our animals, and the stocks I was transporting for First Federal."

"And there's no prize for guessing what riles you up the most," Blain added dryly.

"Why should there be?" Richards countered. "I was entrusted by the bank to see those certificates safely to Tucson."

"You work for the bank, Mr. Richards?" Jessie asked.

He nodded. "Least I did till those damned bandidos—"

"There was no telling they were Mex," Evan interrupted.

"They didn't speak a word of English," Richards protested quickly.

"They didn't speak a word at all," Evan answered.

"And I could see for myself—" Richards began.

Evan looked disgusted. "They wore hats and bandanas. All you could see were their eyes."

"That was enough for me," Richards said pompously.

It was clear Evan disagreed, but he let it slide. "It hardly matters now, anyway," he said with a shrug.

"It will matter a great deal when the authorities set out after them," the bank courier said indignantly.

Jessie noticed Buck's smirk. "What do you think?" she asked him.

Buck laughed dryly. "I think we're all just plum lucky to be alive." Blain and Evan nodded in agreement.

"I just hope we can stay that way," Yvette said softly. There was a fear in her voice that was mirrored in the faces of her companions.

Jessie could understand the concerns of inexperienced travelers who suddenly became stranded. But now that she and Ki had arrived, the dangers seemed over. It would be no problem to guide them to the nearest town. She explained that to them. "Of course you'll have to abandon most of your things."

"Can't we come back for them?" Yvette wondered out loud.

Jessie smiled. "You could, but there'd be no guarantee that they'd still be here when you returned."

The woman wasn't the only one who seemed displeased with the answer. Richards swore under his breath. "Those damned thieves!"

"Not only thieves," Jessie explained patiently. "Any other travels who pass this way would be welcome to help themselves."

"But those are my dresses," Yvette protested.

Jessie shrugged. "Someone traveling through would only see tools, clothing, and supplies that were abandoned. They'd help themselves to what they needed."

"But practically everything I own is in that wagon." Evan sounded stunned.

Ki spoke up for the first time. "But you'd be able to walk away with your most valuable possession." His reference to Evan's very life was not wasted.

Evan nodded. "I was heading west, hoping for a new start. I knew I'd be taking a chance, but I didn't expect to go bust so soon." He looked around at the others. "We were all hoping for a fresh start."

Jessie looked at him sympathetically. "I don't think one setback will be the ruin of you all."

"Then again, Jessie," Ki began, "it's quite possible that

all their possessions will be safe. They've strayed quite a bit off the trail. There may not be anyone passing through here for weeks. I can't be certain, but Little Springs is only a few days' ride east of here."

Jessie started to agree, but was cut short.

"I can't go back there," Yvette cried.

"I agree," Blain said.

Richards elaborated. "We just came from there, Miss Starbuck. None of us want to return like this." They all seemed firm on that.

"I think we'd all rather face what's ahead than turn back in defeat," Evan said bravely.

Jessie thought a moment. "Perhaps there's no need to go back. We're only a few days behind the trail herd, Ki. We could give them some of our food and water, and when we catch up with Ed, send back a few horses just to get them and their wagons to the next outpost."

Everyone liked that idea better. And though Evan stated that he didn't want Jessie to go to any trouble for them, his face showed that he was glad that she was.

Jessie assured them that she couldn't think of not helping them, and then turned to Ki. "Let's divvy up the supplies now, Ki. We still have that herd to catch up with."

"I was thinking of leaving them most of the food, Jessie. We're moving pretty fast, and I don't mind tightening my belt some. . . ."

"Good idea, Ki. There are five of them—"

"Six," Evan interrupted. "We sent my partner out to hunt food." His face looked concerned. "Stephen left yesterday with the other Winchester; he hasn't come back yet."

"Which way did he go?" Ki asked.

Evan pointed north.

"We're heading that way," Jessie said. "If we run into him, we'll give him the good news."

A few minutes later Jessie and Ki were ready to hit the trail.

"Much obliged for your help," Blain said with a smile. Then he bowed stiffly. "Looking forward to seeing you again, ma'am."

As Jessie turned her horse, Yvette looked worried. "We will be okay, won't we?"

Jessie nodded.

"But what if they come back?" Yvette persisted.

"The bandits?"

Yvette nodded.

"They're probably long gone by now," Jessie answered. "And why would they want to come back?" Jessie wasn't expecting an answer, so she thought nothing of the silence that followed. She looked at the group. Blain tried to look suave and charming, Buck seemed indifferent, but Richards seemed very distraught. She started to ask the bank courier about it but stopped herself.

"Don't you worry about us, Jessica," Evan said. "We can take care of ourselves."

Richards's fears could not be contained any longer. "If we could take care of ourselves, we wouldn't be in this mess."

Evan shot him a dirty look. "We'll be all right," he repeated. He was trying to keep up a good front, but he was plainly worried.

Though Jessie didn't think they were in any danger, she couldn't ignore their anxiety. "Ki, maybe you should stay behind."

Ki didn't have a chance to answer before Evan shouted his disapproval. "We couldn't think of letting you travel by yourself."

"I assure you I can take care of myself," Jessie said with a smile.

Evan shook his head and addressed Ki. "Don't even think about it."

Ki agreed. "I know you can take care of yourself, Jessie, but I think these folks will be fine."

Surprisingly, Yvette agreed with both the men. "It's not safe for a woman to be traveling by her lonesome," she insisted. Then she shot a contemptuous look at Richards. "Whatever he's worried might happen to us would happen sooner to a woman out there alone."

Evan had the final word. "If Ki stayed behind, and anything happened to you, I don't think I could ever forgive myself."

His voice was so sincere, and the concern in his eyes so sharp, Jessie couldn't help but feel a strong liking for the man. She gave him a warm smile. "We'll see you folks in a few days." Then with a wave she started her horse towards the north.

As things turned out, their parting lasted only a few hours.

★

Chapter 3

The terrain was slowly changing. The almost solid mat of green grass had turned into a crazy quilt of grass, sand and cacti. Mesquite trees were becoming fewer as creosote and tarbush began to dominate the landscape. Small prickly-pears sporting bright yellow flowers dotted the ground between bush and grass. As a girl Jessie had always liked the way the flower perched on top of the spiny cactus, but as a rancher she grew to dislike the plant. The sharp spines often broke off and got caught in the noses and throats of livestock. She knew her change in attitude was due to the realities and economics of ranching, but just the same, when the mood struck she couldn't help but see the beauty in the flower.

"Thinking about the wagon train back there?" Ki's voice pulled her out of her thoughts.

She shook her head. "Not really."

"You looked deep in thought."

"I was letting my mind wander."

"So was I," Ki continued. "And there's something I don't quite understand about that group."

"They're an odd bunch," Jessie agreed.

"It's more than just that. They all seemed to be afraid of something."

"No one likes getting robbed and left for dead."

"No." He thought some more on it. "I guess it's none of our business anyway."

Jessie let out a laugh. "Do I detect an air of only casual interest, Ki?"

He looked offended. "Is there something wrong with that?"

"Of course not," Jessie said playfully, "but I notice you're considerably less critical and less curious in situations that don't represent any direct danger to us."

Ki gave her a stern look. "You can never be certain a situation does not represent any danger," he said seriously. "But having said that, I guess you're right. It's only a passing interest. They do make an odd bunch, though."

"An odd bunch or an odd couple?" Ki didn't catch Jessie's drift. "You were no doubt wondering about Miss DeVeau and Mr. Strummer," she teased playfully.

Ki smiled back. "No more than you."

Jessie was wondering how to wipe that smug smile off Ki's face when she saw something in the distance. "Ki," she said suddenly and pointed.

She put her horse into a gallop, and a minute later she was jumping down to stand beside the body of a man sprawled facedown in a tarbush. She rolled the body over just as Ki rushed up with a canteen.

"It's too late for that," Jessie said. "He's already dead."

"Water would never have saved him. Look." Ki pointed to the man's side. The body was caked in dirt, but there were two small patches that were of a darker brown. It was the dark brown of crusty blood.

"He's been shot to death," Jessie observed.

"Why, and by whom?" Ki wondered.

Jessie stood up. "At least we know who he is."

Ki nodded. "There's not much doubt about it."

Jessie pointed to the rifle that lay a few inches from the body. "And that Winchester makes it almost certain." She paused a moment, then continued. "Maybe we're making a big mistake, Ki."

"You're not referring to his identity." It was not a question.

"I'm thinking of that odd bunch back there."

Ki nodded. "Let me have a quick look around, then I'll throw him over one of the horses."

On the way back to the wagons, Jessie and Ki each raised many questions, none of which they could answer. Jessie summed it up best: "There's a lot more going on than meets the eye."

"Then we'll have to look that much closer," was Ki's response.

Their return met with much surprise. Then, as the reason for their return became clear, the prevailing attitude quickly changed to anger and fear. Only Evan showed sorrow. Perhaps that was natural. Evan knew the man well, while the others were virtual strangers. They feared more what the dead man represented than the fact that he was dead. But even Evan's sorrow soon turned to anger.

"They won't get away with this," he raged. "They can steal from us and rob us, and leave us for dead, but I won't let them butcher us one by one."

"Who are they?" Jessie asked.

Evan ignored the question. "If I have to spend the rest of my life looking for them, they won't get away with it."

Yvette tried to calm him, but it was clear she was also

agitated. She was also very scared, and her words did little to soothe him.

"They shot him dead, just like a dog," Evan hissed. "They let him die out there with not even a proper burial. The buzzards would have picked his bones clean. It ain't a Christian thing to do."

"And what you're thinking of doing to them isn't any better," Jessie said softly.

"They can't be allowed to get away with this."

"They won't," Jessie promised. "But there's little you can do right now."

"I can give him a decent burying—and a simple prayer to send him on his way." With that he went to the wagon and returned a minute later with a shovel. Ki stood up to help.

"Thanks, Ki, but I think I'd like to do this by myself. We've come a long way together, me and Stephen, and I'd like these last few moments to be alone with him."

Ki understood and sat back down on his heels.

There was little conversation. Some of them picked at their food; others sipped at their coffee. When Evan finally returned his emotions had stabilized. He joined the group and sat down. "I reckon this changes things somewhat."

"The crazy bastards'll keep coming back till they kill us all," Richards whined.

Blain nodded. "It doesn't seem like they high-tailed it out of here after all, does it?"

"We can't just sit around and wait for them," Yvette said nervously. "We'll all die out here."

"Listen," Jessie began sharply, "we're all safe. There are only six of them. There are six of us."

Buck spoke out. "I count five—four, seein' as how your friend there ain't packin' an iron."

Jessie smiled. "Ki doesn't need a gun to be deadly. And

I count myself. I can shoot." She wondered which was the greater understatement.

"Ma'am, I don't mean to scoff, but—"

"With any luck we won't have to prove either of those statements. And if we do, I'll let you make up your own mind. But I don't think you'll be calling me a liar."

It was Blain's turn now. "I ain't doubting you, but even so that's six against six. Even odds. When a man's life is on the line he likes to be looking at something better than an even chance."

"As long as we keep calm we'll have the advantage," Ki answered. "We're all safe, provided we don't lose our heads. We'll post guards tonight . . ."

"And what about tomorrow, and the next night, and the night after that?" Richards asked nervously.

"Tomorrow we'll all head north. My trail crew is only a few days ahead of us."

"We can't walk the whole way," Yvette protested.

"I've walked farther," Ki said simply.

"So have I," added Jessie. "We have four horses. There are seven of us. The women can double up with a man, and the odd man out can take turns walking." Jessie then went into a little more detail. No one seemed totally pleased with the plan, but there was no argument. After all, there was no better alternative.

"We should all try and get a good night's sleep," Ki said finally. "I'll take the first watch."

Jessie suspected that Ki would be the first and only one to stand guard. He was quite capable of spending the whole night on full alert. Still, as she went to get her bedroll she made a quiet suggestion to him. "If you need a few hours' sleep don't hesitate to wake me, Ki."

He nodded and said good-night.

23

• • •

The moon slid behind a large cloud, and the night grew considerably darker. For a moment, but only a brief moment, Ki thought it was the wind that he heard. He listened closely. The horses stirred. That was not unusual. Then he heard the muffled step—a man walking slowly, trying to keep silent.

Ki got up quickly, reaching into his pocket for a *shuriken* as he did so. In Ki's hands the silver throwing star was as deadly as any bullet from a gun. But it was a whole lot quieter. And that noiseless accuracy had often saved Ki's life. Many times Ki found it necessary to dispose of one assailant without making his presence known. While the crack of a gun would give away his position, the hushed whir of the *shuriken* in flight would go unheard. Even if someone heard the soft, deadly sound, its detection, and the realization of what it represented, always came too late.

Suddenly Ki stopped. He thought he heard another set of footsteps circling outside the perimeter of the wagons. Then the wind changed direction and Ki couldn't be certain. After listening another moment, Ki decided that, if anything, the sound was nothing more than a footstep bouncing off the side of one of the wagons. Even with only a gentle breeze blowing in the thin night, air sounds and directions were often deceiving.

Then the steps began again. It was clear now that the man was moving towards the line where the horses were tethered.

Ki let a grin form on his face. Had any outsider tried to approach the wagons, Ki would have heard him sooner. A man could not have gotten this close without being detected. The fact that he heard this intruder once he was already behind the wagons meant only one thing. The man was not an intruder at all. He was part of the wagon party. But that fact made him no less dangerous, and Ki did not

24

relax his guard, even slightly. On the contrary, he inched the *shuriken* between his thumb and index finger, balancing it for a fast throw.

He didn't know who he was stalking, but he had a pretty good idea why. Someone in the group had decided that he would stand a better chance on his own, and to that end was now making his way to the horses. How badly that man wished to succeed would determine Ki's next action. It was likely that once discovered, the man, though embarrassed and ashamed, would give up on his plan of escape and go back to his wagon. But there was no guarantee of that. It was equally possible that the man would choose to fight. In the eventuality that the man would shoot first and ask questions later, Ki was prepared.

Still, he was surprised by what happened next. He was about to call out to the man and order him to back away from the horses, when a figure dove out from behind one of the tethered animals and knocked the hopeful escapee to the ground. There was a startled scream as the man went down, arms and legs flailing.

It took eight steps for Ki to reach the two men, but by then the fight was already over, if in fact it could be called a fight at all. Buck was well-built, powerful, and a seasoned fighter. Jim Richards, slight of build and timid of spirit, didn't stand a chance, even if he hadn't been taken by surprise. Buck hauled a scared Richards to his feet and, holding the clerk's shirt in his left hand, slapped the man's face with the back of his right. He was just about to strike again when Ki interceded.

Ki shot out his arm and grabbed Buck's wrist before it could land a second blow. "There's no need for that," he said calmly.

Buck turned, first surprised, then angered. "Mind yer own business," he snapped, as he struggled to free his wrist from Ki's grip.

Ki released his hold. The second he did so, Buck swung a left at Ki's head. Ki saw it coming from the corner of his eye, but Buck acted so quickly there was no time to block or dodge. The best Ki could do was move with the punch. The fist connected in front of the ear, and though it knocked Ki off his feet, it did little damage. There was plenty of power behind it. Buck was the type of fighter who knew how to put his bulk behind one of his blows, but Ki was already in motion before the fist landed against his head. That was the reason he lost his footing. That was also the reason the powerful punch was only a glancing blow.

Ki got to his feet quickly, but Buck had already turned his attention back to Richards. Apparently, he had taken Ki for a one-punch knockout, and was again grabbing for the bank clerk. "Where was you runnin' off to?" he asked angrily as he landed a punch to the man's stomach.

"That's enough," Ki ordered. He didn't expect Buck to comply simply because he was told to, but he did expect the man's fury would be redirected. Ki wasn't wrong.

"I'll teach you to stick yer nose where it don't belong," Buck said as he swung another fist in Ki's direction.

But this time Ki was prepared. He brought up a forearm to block the punch, then lashed out with a *mae-geri-keage*. Ki's foot connected with Buck's solar plexus, and the man doubled over. But the fight wasn't out of him yet. Head down, clutching his stomach, he rushed at Ki.

Ki sidestepped, then, with a quick chop to Buck's back, dropped the man in the dirt.

Meanwhile, Richards had not been idle. When Ki turned to him he already had a saddle thrown over one of the horses. "I didn't save you from Buck so you could run off," Ki explained simply. He didn't think he'd have to use force with the man, but he wasn't ruling out the possibility.

"You can't stop me," Richards answered, and Ki noticed the small derringer the clerk held in his hand.

"Put that away before someone gets hurt."

"Stand where you are and you won't get hurt," Richards warned.

"I wasn't thinking of myself," Ki said bluntly. "You can't mount up and keep that gun trained on me."

"Shut up," Richards snapped.

"The minute you grab hold of the saddle, I'll be on top of you."

"Don't try anything." Richards's voice was shaky. It was clear he had his doubts. But then an idea struck him. "Turn around," he commanded.

Ki looked him straight in the eye. "You can't shoot a man in the back."

"Turn around," he repeated.

Ki hesitated. He wasn't afraid of being shot, and he was pretty certain that that was not the clerk's intention. But once his back was turned he couldn't be sure when to make his move. He could listen and take his chances, but there was much room for error. The man's ability to shoot was an unknown, but it didn't take much skill to shoot a derringer. It wasn't worth the risk.

Ki's other alternative was to wait it out. He still had the *shuriken*. When Richards thought he was safely away, the throwing star could still be brought into use. Ki didn't favor the idea, though. He had no doubts that he could bring down the man; the question was at what cost. He wouldn't be able to accurately pick his target. A non-lethal wound to the shoulderblade was only inches from a deadly wound to the neck. There was no reason to risk killing Richards. Certainly the man's crime of cowardice and desertion did not warrant execution. There had to be a better way.

"You're making a big mistake," Ki said patiently.

27

"You do as I say," Richards answered. The gun was shaking nervously in his hand.

Ki continued. "You'll stand a better chance sticking it out with us than trying to go it alone out there."

"I'll decide that for myself. Now turn around," Richards said impatiently.

"It will be you, one man alone, against all those bandidos. You won't make it."

Ki had pushed too far. Richards was through discussing. "You turn around now or I'll shoot you where you stand, so help me."

"Easy," Ki began calmly. "I'll do just as you—" He never finished his sentence. He was struck below his knees and toppled to the ground. The sharp pop of the derringer echoed in the night as his face hit the dirt.

Ki felt the weight on top of his legs. He struggled to roll over onto his side, moving enough to free his arm. He swung his right fist in a large arc, connecting with something hard and solid as it went around. The weight shifted slightly and Ki, still pinned, rolled onto his back.

Buck was on top of Ki and was bringing both hands up over his head, ready to strike. Ki acted quickly, chopping the side of his hand into Buck's kidney. The man let out a gasp and dropped his hands to his side.

Ki then grabbed his opponent's lapels and, with the assistance of a knee to the back, rolled the man over his head.

Ki scrambled to his feet in time to see Richards riding away. Buck, just as quickly, also saw the bank clerk escaping. He drew his revolver and leveled it.

Ki launched himself into the air. A moment later his feet slammed down solidly between Buck's shoulders. The man pitched forward. The gun exploded, the bullet biting harmlessly into the dirt.

Ki grabbed for the revolver and wrenched it away from

a startled Buck. He tossed it into the distance and was about to face Buck when Jessie came running up.

"What's going on?" she asked quickly.

Buck turned, confused. The Colt that Jessie held in her hand settled his moment of indecision.

"You all right, Ki?" she continued.

Ki nodded. Evan and Blain now were rushing up, also demanding to know what was going on. "We heard a shot." Evan began.

"Have him explain," Ki said with a nod to Buck. "I have to retrieve one of our horses."

"I could have shot him," Buck said angrily.

"There was no need for that; he won't get far," Ki said.

"The skunk deserved it, sneakin' out on us."

"Ki . . .?" Jessie began.

"Stay here. I'll be back shortly." And with that Ki hopped onto the back of one of the horses and took off into the night.

Chapter 4

Ki didn't bother looking for any signs, though it was bright enough. The moon had come out from behind the clouds, and if Ki had had to, he could have dropped to his knees to study the ground for fresh tracks, but he didn't think it would be necessary. He had seen the direction Richards rode off in, and had a strong suspicion the man would not veer from his course. Having left Buck and Ki fighting it out on the ground, Richards would not be expecting pursuit. But more importantly, Ki judged the man to be the type who believed that the fastest way between two points was a straight line. Plainly, the bank clerk wanted to put as much distance between himself and the wagon camp as possible.

Ki was also betting his horsemanship against that of Richards. Though Ki was riding bareback, his strong legs gripped the flanks of the horse, and his fingers locked themselves in the horse's mane. His body moved fluidly with the animal. Despite the darkness and the rocky soil he pushed his horse at a full gallop.

Minutes later he caught sight of the figure up ahead. Richards was moving at a slow trot, but even so he seemed to be having trouble staying in the saddle. Ki closed the distance, and Richards turned at the sound of pounding hooves. Even from afar Ki could see the stricken expression on the man's face.

Richards spurred his horse to a gallop. The animal bolted forward and after a few paces Richards had to drop his hands to the saddlehorn. That was when his troubles began. The extra weight he placed on the horn altered the balance and the saddle started to shift to the side. Panicked, Richards leaned to the opposite side, using the stirrup to help change his position. As his foot straightened and pressed down against the stirrup iron, the saddle shifted even more. Richards hung precariously half in and half out of the saddle. A better rider might have stood a chance, but for the bank teller it was only a matter of time. His time came seconds later.

Ki watched it happen. The saddle rotated around the animal's back and Richards was catapulted right off the horse. He fell cleanly to the ground, and though he hit hard, he was lucky that neither leg got caught up in the stirrups. Ki was not surprised it had happened. In fact he was expecting some such development, and in truth was surprised it had not happened sooner.

While Ki and Buck were engaged in their fight, Richards had had only a few seconds to enact his getaway. There was hardly enough time to rig the saddle properly. An experienced rider like Jessie might have done it, and a competent ranch hand might have done a fair job, but Ki doubted Richards could do the job properly in the short time he had. There were a bunch of mistakes that could have been made. The one that did Richards in was the cinch. He had failed to tighten the girth properly, and given time and pressure the saddle eventually slipped.

Ki charged past the fallen rider and caught up with the loose horse. He grabbed the animal's reins and circled back to where Richards was just picking himself up from the dirt.

The bank teller eyed Ki with fear and apprehension. "Don't hurt me," he pleaded.

Ki remained on his horse, saying nothing as he looked down on the man. His silence only served to upset Richards more.

"I never planned to shoot you," Richards continued. "I never shot anyone in my life," he added quickly.

"You shouldn't carry a gun, even a derringer, if you don't plan to use it," Ki stated plainly.

Richards smiled nervously. "You're damned right. A fellow like me got no business carrying a gun. You taught Jim Richards an important lesson today," he said as he reached into his pocket. Ki moved his horse closer as the teller continued. "I got no need for this anymore," he said as he pulled out the small derringer.

The look in the man's eyes alerted Ki instantly. He reacted quickly. Unhampered by a stirrup, Ki's right leg swung up and out, and crashed into Richards's outstretched arm. The derringer exploded, then dropped, as Richards clutched at his bruised arm.

"My arm," he cried out in pain. "It feels like it's broken."

Ki was unsympathetic. "When you get wherever you're going, have a doctor take a look at it." He turned the horses and started off.

"Wait! Where are you going?" Richards cried.

"Back to camp."

"You can't leave me here," the bank teller whined.

Ki stopped the horse. "As I recall, you were in quite a hurry to go thataway. . . ."

"But you can't leave me," Richards repeated.

"You've tried to shoot me twice," Ki reminded him. "Anyone who wants to go that badly, I won't try to stop."

"Then why'd you come after me?"

Ki tilted his head towards the other horse. "That's Starbuck property. It belongs to Jessie."

"It's murder to leave me here alone."

Ki shrugged.

Richards looked desperate. "For pity's sake, wait."

"Perhaps if you tell me why you had to sneak away in the middle of the night . . .?"

"It wasn't my idea."

"No?"

"It was Buck. He told me our only chance was to get away tonight."

"It didn't look like you were friends."

"He tried to double-cross me." Ki looked doubtful. "I wouldn't lie to you."

Ki laughed dryly. "You've tried to shoot me."

"But I wouldn't lie to you. Honest." Richards hesitated, then seemed to decide. He continued, "He tried to cross me for my money." The bank teller held up a leather satchel that was slung across his shoulder.

"There's money in there?"

Richards nodded enthusiastically, then brightened, misunderstanding Ki's interest.

"It's not really money, but it's just as good. Negotiable bonds."

"How did Buck know you had those bonds?"

"I don't know. But there's enough here for both of us. I'll cut you in. Just give me that horse."

"Where'd the bonds come from?" Ki asked.

34

"I'll give you a quarter share." Ki seemed uninterested. Richards upped his offer. "A third."

"I don't need your money," Ki stated tersely.

"An even split, fifty-fifty," Richards said frantically. "Do you realize how much I'm offering you?"

Ki shook his head. "No."

"More than you'd make in ten years. Certainly more than that horse is worth."

"You're wasting your time," Ki informed him.

"No one will ever know. It's night, I had a head start on you. I could have easily gotten away."

"But you didn't."

"They'll never know you caught me, they'll never know you let me go."

"I'm not interested," Ki said.

"Then if you don't want the money for yourself, consider it as a sale. I'd like to buy that horse from your employer. I'm willing to pay a hundred times what it's worth."

"You better save your money, Richards. Out there you'll need every dollar of it. Food and water are hard to come by."

When Ki returned to the camp everyone was up and waiting. Buck had already given his side of the story, telling how he had heard Richards sneak around to the horses and how he had tried to stop the man, and would have if it weren't for Ki's interference. Ki chose not to retell any of Richards's version.

In fact he was unusually silent. When Buck turned to him and badgered him for letting Richards escape, Ki said nothing. Then when Blain called Buck a fool for not noticing that Ki returned with an extra horse, Ki still said nothing. It wasn't until Jessie thanked Ki for retrieving the horse that Ki even mentioned the bank teller.

"Richards is walking in behind me," he said flatly. "He should be here in a few minutes."

"I reckon there's no purpose served by us all standin' around like this," Evan announced. The others nodded, and one by one they headed back to their wagons. Evan turned to Ki. "If you'd like I can stand watch the rest of the night."

Ki thanked him but declined the offer.

"Your mind set, Ki? I don't think I'll get back to sleep."

"You'll need the rest," Ki answered. "And I'll be fine."

Evan nodded and left.

Jessie moved alongside Ki. "You seem rather short-tempered," she said gently.

"I do, don't I," he agreed.

"Any ideas why?"

"I've been punched, knocked down, shot at twice."

"Nothing unusual there," Jessie said with a trace of a smile.

"And offered a bribe."

Ki's last words sparked Jessie's interest. "By who? Richards?"

Ki nodded, and told her what happened.

"Do you believe any of Richards's story?" Jessie asked when he finished.

"The man's a liar. There's no doubt about that. But then, Buck is no angel, either."

"You think there might be some truth to it, then?"

Ki shook his head. "But what's the difference?"

"Ki, this doesn't sound like you."

Ki started to speak, then stopped.

"Are you all right? I'm worried about you," Jessie said with concern.

"I'm fine, Jessie, but I can't help wondering if after tonight any of this is worth it."

"You've been shot at before, and you've certainly had more than your share of fights. . . ."

"Yes, but never with or by people I was trying to help."

"I see," Jessie said thoughtfully.

"There's something strange about the whole lot of them, and I can't help but think that whatever trouble they've gotten into they more than likely deserve."

"It's unlike you to play judge and jury. And after that speech you gave me at the house about helping people."

Ki softened. "I guess that's it, Jessie. There are people out there, honest, hard-working people, that really need help. And we're wasting our time here."

"It's not totally by choice. We didn't plan on this, but all the same we can't turn our backs on these people."

A smile formed on his face, but his tone was serious. "You better not, or you might wind up with a knife in it."

"A poor attempt at humor," Jessie remarked casually. "You must be feeling better."

"Not really. I'm also thinking about what brought us out here in the first place."

"I haven't forgotten either, but the trail herd will have to wait till we can get these folks to safety."

"I figured you'd feel that way."

"Don't you?" Jessie pressed.

"Let's say right now I'd rather save a head of good Texas longhorn than a Jim Richards, or a Buck."

"Tomorrow, after some sleep, you'll feel different." Ki was about to protest, but Jessie cut him short. "I'll keep the watch till morning. It's only a few hours more."

Just then they heard someone approach through the darkness. "Don't shoot, it's me," the voice said.

"It's all right, Mr. Richards," Jessie answered.

"I'm glad it's you," he began. "That crazy Ki knocked me down and made me walk all—" He stopped abruptly as he got closer and saw Ki.

"You better get some sleep," Jessie told the bank clerk coldly. Then she turned to Ki. "I see what you mean."

"Not even worth a single calf," Ki muttered.

"Good night, Ki."

Ki took Jessie's advice, and headed for his bedroll.

"It's just me."

"Evan?"

"Jessie? I thought Ki was standing guard."

"We switched," she said simply.

As Evan moved close to her Jessie could see he was slightly embarrassed. "If you need to tell him something . . . ?" Jessie began.

"Oh, no," Evan said quickly. "It's just that I don't think it's proper for me to, ah, well just us two alone . . ."

Jessie smiled. "Don't worry. I won't mention it to Yvette."

Evan now seemed not only flustered but confused as well. "Well what I mean is . . ."

His words trailed off, and Jessie didn't push. "But you did come out here for a reason?"

Evan nodded. "Like I expected, I couldn't sleep. I thought maybe I'd walk out to Stephen's grave. Spend some time with him before we move on tomorrow. I know there's no real point to it, but like I said, I couldn't sleep. Anyway I just wanted to tell Ki, so I wouldn't surprise him."

"He'd have heard you."

Evan smiled. "I reckon surprise wasn't the best word. I think I wanted to let him know so I wouldn't get shot at."

Jessie laughed. "Ki doesn't wear a gun."

"He seems to do all right without one."

Jessie agreed.

"He's a good man," Evan noted.

Again Jessie agreed, but the tone in Evan's voice had

38

her a little confused. Normally she would take this opportunity to explain her relationship with Ki. If Evan were single and had shown some interest in her, perhaps she would have; but to do so now, she feared, would be too forward. Jessie did not respond, and an uncomfortable moment of silence passed between them.

"The moon is almost as bright as a lantern," Evan remarked at length.

"Bright enough to blot out most of the stars in the sky," Jessie added.

The exchange was over quickly and the awkward silence returned. Evan tried again on another tack. "You don't mind staying up the rest of the night?" he asked Jessie.

"Someone has to do it," she answered with a smile.

"It's really not all that important to stand over Stephen's grave. If you'd like some company. . .?"

"I would very much," she said quickly.

Evan continued. "I mean he was my friend and he keeps runnin' through my mind, but me standin' out there won't change anything."

"No, it won't," Jessie agreed. "Why don't we sit," she said as she pointed to the ground.

Evan hunkered down on his heels, leaning forward across his raised knees, while Jessie sat with her legs crossed Indian style.

"I guess what bothers me most is the thought of Stephen getting gunned down defenseless. Murdered in cold blood."

"I know it's no consolation, but I don't think it happened like that," Jessie began.

"What do you mean? How do you know?"

"After we found Stephen, Ki had a look around. If anything your friend tried to be a hero."

"I don't understand."

39

"It seems he stumbled across the outlaws and tried to ambush them."

"What makes you say that?" Evan said with surprise.

"Certain signs. Stephen was lying in a bush when we found him. He was probably using it for cover. He was shot in his side, from someone coming up on his flank. Fifty yards away there were the ashes of a campfire and tracks of six horses."

"The bandits?"

Jessie nodded and continued. "There was a lot of scurrying around, too, as if they were taken by surprise. There was also a bloodstain on a rock. Stephen at least wounded one of them."

"And you can tell all this just by looking around?"

She nodded. "Sometimes you can even tell the color of the shirt a man is wearing and the type of tobacco he's smoking," Jessie said teasingly.

It took a minute for Evan to realize she was pulling his leg, but then a warm smile spread over his face. "I reckon I have a lot to learn about this sort of thing."

Jessie was curious about where he was from, and asked.

"St. Joe. My folks were from Minnesota." It only took a little prodding to get him to tell her about his family, his childhood on the farm, and his endless desire to head out West. The first leg of the journey took him to St. Joseph, where he spent a few years working for a shipping company, saving his money. He also told Jessie about the woman he'd left behind in that city. A woman who didn't share his dreams of the open opportunity and ready wealth that lay waiting somewhere out in the open country.

At that point Evan fell silent. He seemed to want some affirmation of his dream. Jessie smiled. "The roads aren't paved with gold," she said gently. "But there is plenty of opportunity for those who are willing to work for it."

"I was certainly willing to try, but, depending how we

come out of this, I may be cleaned out. I'd hate to have to go back to St. Joe and start all over again. . . ." His words trailed off, but a moment later he continued, his voice firm and resolute. "But if I have to start all over again, dang it, I will."

"That's the spirit," Jessie said with honest admiration.

"I'm a little smarter this time, I know my way around, and it won't take nearly as long to get up enough money."

"But I wouldn't count this trip a bust yet, Evan."

"Damn near," he said without thinking. Then he blushed. "Pardon my language, Jessie."

"I've heard much worse. In fact," she added with a smile of her own, "I've said much worse."

"It must have been hard for a young girl to grow up out here," Evan remarked. "You were raised out here, weren't you?"

Jessie nodded, and began telling Evan about her life. She neglected to tell him about the extent of the Starbuck empire, and of her battles with the international cartel that had tried to destroy that empire. She did tell him, though, about her father and the Circle Star.

"You seem to know about a lot more than just ranching," Evan said.

"There's a lot to running a ranch," Jessie answered. "It's not just raising cattle. These days you have to deal with shipping, railroads, the market, not to mention the banks. And then more and more ranchers are becoming aware of breeding and the possibilities of cross-breeding." She started to talk about a strain of cattle that had recently been brought over from England, then stopped abruptly. "I'm sorry. I don't mean to bore you with all this."

"Oh, you're not," Evan assured her.

"You're just being polite," Jessie said with a smile. "The point, though, is that the days of having a few

41

hundred head of cattle and taking them to the town auction are gone."

"You don't seem any worse for it."

"You have to change and expand with the times," Jessie answered. "And it isn't boring," she added with a smile.

"You don't mind spending all your time in one place? That's what made me crazy as a kid. My whole world was the few acres my parents worked."

Jessie laughed and told him about some of her travels. Of course many of the stories included Ki.

"You've known Ki a long time," Evan noted.

"Since I was a little girl."

Something in Evan's face changed. "Then he's just a friend," he said cautiously.

"Not just. He's a very special friend and companion."

"But you don't, ah, I mean, you're not . . ."

"No, we're not lovers," Jessie said simply. Hope and excitement blossomed all over Evan's face. "But I don't see how that's a concern of yours."

Evan was stung badly by her words. "No, I reckon it isn't," he muttered. "Forgive me for letting my imagination get the best of me. I just thought for a moment that maybe there was something between us. . . ."

Jessie toned down her rebuke. Possibly she was equally guilty for encouraging him. Undeniably, she found him an attractive man. "Evan, when I said I wouldn't mention our meeting to Yvette I didn't mean to have you take it as an invite to—"

Evan broke into a hearty laugh. "Yvette! You think that we're together?"

"Aren't you?"

"I first laid eyes on her a week ago in Little Springs. She was traveling alone, and joined up with us."

"A lot can happen in a week," Jessie countered.

"Jessie, she sleeps on one side of the wagon and me and

Stephen sleep on the other. And there's a sheet hanging between us," he added for emphasis, then laughed again loudly.

"Shush," Jessie warned. "You'll wake everyone."

"Let's take a walk," Evan suggested.

"You forget, I'm standing guard," Jessie reminded him.

"You can watch just as well from that mesquite. And we can talk more freely over there."

"And that's all you want to do, talk?" Jessie said with a twinkle in her eye.

Evan didn't answer. He extended his arm, and taking her hand in his, led her away from the wagons to the distant tree.

Chapter 5

Evan pulled Jessie into his arms and crushed his lips against hers. She offered no resistance, and her lips, soft and warm, had an eagerness all their own.

After a time Evan pulled back. "I really did want to come over here to talk," he said sheepishly. "I don't know what came over me."

"You have an odd style of conversation," Jessie remarked. "Let's talk some more," she added with a smile.

Evan needed no further encouragement. He took hold of her cheek and tilted her head back slightly before lowering his lips to hers. This time their embrace lasted even longer. Evan's tongue caressed Jessie's as his free hand roamed over her back. Slowly his mouth moved from hers and he covered her soft cheeks with baby kisses. "I've wanted to do this to you ever since I laid eyes on you."

"Is that all you've wanted to do, Evan?"

"I can't even mention the rest," he said shyly.

"Then show me," Jessie whispered.

Evan lowered his head to her neck and kissed his way down to her shoulder, pushing back her shirt as his lips moved along the softness of her skin. Jessie let out a sigh.

"I've spent a lot of time thinking about you, Jessie. There's a whole lot I want to do . . ." He began to unbutton her blouse. Slowly, one button at a time.

"We have till morning, Evan. That should be enough time."

"Barely," he answered with a smile. His fingers traced light patterns over her bare skin as he exposed her body.

"If you don't think you'll have enough time, maybe you shouldn't tarry?" Jessie suggested.

Evan smiled. "Are you in a hurry?"

Jessie shook her head. "Maybe I should lie down."

Evan quickly removed his shirt and spread it out on the ground. Jessie lay down on top of it, and Evan lowered himself next to her. His chest was broad and muscular, and was covered with curls of light brown hair. Jessie began running her hands over his chest then lowered her mouth to his nipple. She sucked at it teasingly, before he pulled away.

"You don't like that?" Jessie asked.

"It tickles," Evan answered.

"Doesn't it feel good?"

"You tell me," Evan said as he brushed back her shirt and lowered his mouth to her nipple. He sucked the red bud into his mouth, and Jessie let out an appreciative sigh.

Evan lifted his head, but only briefly, to move to her other nipple. He let his tongue run circles around her breast, eventually narrowing in on her stiff bud.

Jessie ran her fingers through his hair, and pressed his head into her firm breast. Evan sucked harder on her pointed bud, and a deep moan escaped from Jessie's lips.

Evan shifted his weight and placed a leg between hers. Unconsciously Jessie began to gyrate her hips, pressing against his strong body. She became increasingly aware of the spreading warmth that was concentrated in her loins. She reached out for and found the large bulge between Evan's legs. She began to stroke it purposefully, and was not surprised when, a few moments later, Evan pulled away and stood up.

He quickly undid his belt buckle, then pushed his pants down to his knees. His pole stood out at rigid attention, and Jessie popped up to her knees to take his erection in her hands. She brushed it against her soft cheeks, then caressed its length with her warm tongue.

Evan let out a gasp. "You're making it very hard. . . ."

"It's already hard," Jessie noted with satisfaction.

"For a man to take off his boots," Evan finished in a husky voice.

"Would you like me to stop?" she asked as she engulfed his shaft with her mouth.

She took his moan as a positive sign and continued her ministrations. Her tongue flicked over the satin-smooth tip, while her hands firmly stroked the rock-hard shaft.

Evan continued to try and remove his boots but it was no use. Jessie's mouth remained glued to his pole, and soon he had forgotten all about his feet.

Jessie started to suck hungrily on his rod, teasing him still with her flicking tongue.

Evan started to protest. "Jessie, I think you better stop."

"Do you really think that?" she said shrewdly, and without waiting for an answer, relaxed her throat and lowered her mouth to the base of his shaft. His knees trembled and she could imagine the shudder of pleasure that ran through his whole body.

Gradually she withdrew her head, until only her lips were pressed lightly against his tip, then she repeated her action sucking him deeply down her throat.

Again Evan protested, but this time only half-heartedly.

While he was begging her to stop, his hips were rocking back and forth.

Jessie withdrew her mouth, but replaced it with her hand. "I'll stop if you really want me too, Evan, but there's no reason to." She moved her hand back and forth along his slippery shaft. A loud groan was the only response he could muster.

She tightened her grip and worked her hand faster. Evan moaned appreciatively louder, and Jessie once more took him inside her mouth.

He dropped his hands to her head, and wrapped his fingers in her tawny locks. His hips were moving of their own volition as Jessie worked her magic on his throbbing member.

Jessie wrapped her arms around his hips and grabbed his muscular buttocks. She dug her fingers into his firm flesh and he tensed his body in time to her bobbing head.

She could feel him growing larger in her mouth. She didn't need his faint warning to know he was close to climaxing.

"Jessie, if you don't stop now it'll be too late," he began faintly.

His words only excited her more. She ran her teeth gently over his pole, and he let out a soft cry.

"Jessie . . . !"

But it was too late. His hips clenched and bucked forward, his pole twitched, and his muscle spasmed strongly, sending his seed down Jessie's waiting throat.

Jessie was prepared, but the sheer volume of his fluid made her gag. She swallowed and caught her breath.

"I'm sorry, Jessie, I didn't mean to . . ."

"There's no need to apologize," she said seriously. "I'm a big girl, Evan. I knew what was going to happen," she added with a smile.

"But I didn't mean to make it, ah, uncomfortable for you. Maybe I shouldn't have . . ."

"Nonsense. I just wasn't prepared for so much," she said seductively.

"I reckon it has been a while at that," he said with a sheepish smile. "Mind if I take my boots off now?"

"As long as you take mine off too."

In a snap, Evan had shed his boots and pants, then dropped to his knees to remove Jessie's clothing. As he pulled off her tight-fitting jeans he emitted a sigh of approval. "You're beautiful," he said simply.

He ran his fingers up her smooth leg, feeling the muscular firmness yet feminine softness of her velvety thigh. She parted her legs to his touch and soon his fingers were lost in a patch of moist, downy curls. His fingers traced the damp folds of her womanhood, and now it was Jessie's turn to moan.

"I want to make you feel as good as you made me feel," he said gently.

"I'm sure you will," Jessie said as she moved her hips to meet his exploring fingers.

He leaned over to rub his cheek against the roundness of her bosom.

"Oh, your beard," Jessie exclaimed.

Evan immediately pulled back. "Sorry, Jessie. I wasn't thinking. When you don't shave every day you forget how rough it can feel. Especially against your soft, soft skin."

"No, it feels good," she said as she pulled his head back down to her breast. "Tickles."

Instinctively his lips found their way to her pointing nipple, and he sucked the red bud back into his mouth. His fingers continued to press between her legs and as his palm flattened out against her mound, his finger slid into her softness.

49

Jessie let another moan escape from her lips, and Evan began to work his finger in and out of her.

"It feels good," she whispered in his ear. "But don't tease me . . ."

Evan brought his head up to her neck. "I don't plan to," he said as he nibbled on her ear. "At least no more than you teased me."

She started to protest, but her words trailed off into a soft moan, as his fingers found her swollen pleasure center. His gentle touch, almost unbearably light, only increased her desire. "I don't want your finger," she finally managed to say, "I want you."

Evan moved his finger in slow sensual circles, alternately applying pressure, then releasing. "You don't really want me to stop," he said in mock imitation of her own words just a few minutes earlier. "I will if you want me to, but . . ."

Jessie knew it was pointless to try and convince him with her words. Instead she slid her hand down his body. She was pleasantly surprised to find his shaft already hard and throbbing. She stroked it lightly, knowing full well that Evan would not be able to resist long. He increased the pressure of his fingers, and she stroked his rod faster.

He groaned softly. "You win, Jessie," he said with a laugh, then rolled on top of her.

Jessie let out a gasp. She knew he was large, but she hadn't realized just how large he was till he slid into her. But the initial discomfort turned to pleasure as he slowly moved in and out of her.

Jessie wrapped her arms around his broad shoulders, and brought her legs up around his hips. She pressed her body close to his, drawing him deep inside of her.

"I never imagined you would feel this good," Evan said in a throaty whisper.

Jessie laughed. "Maybe you don't have a good imagination."

"It's just that it's never been this good before."

Jessie lifted her head slightly to be able to kiss his mouth. As her tongue slid into his mouth his solid shaft thrust with more urgency.

Jessie mirrored his every move, and soon her breath was coming in quick gasps. Evan, too, was breathing heavily, as his hips pumped into her.

She felt herself rushing headlong towards ecstasy. "Don't hold back," she urged Evan, as she nibbled on his neck.

Evan's answer came in the form of short, repeated thrusts. He lifted up on his elbows, and rocked his hips quickly.

Jessie felt her body tense: first her calves, then her thighs; then she stretched her legs out straight. Her pelvis lifted to meet Evan's probing shaft. Her stomach tensed and her breasts jutted forward. A warm glow spread over her body, intensifying somewhere deep inside her.

Suddenly Evan lowered his weight and thrust deep inside of her. Jessie let out a gasp; a tremor swept through her. Again Evan plunged the full length of his rod deep inside of her, and the first of many spasms wracked her body.

Jessie let out a small scream as her body seemed to explode. Her eyes closed, and her head rolled back, as her body released again and again.

Finally her body relaxed, her breathing returned to normal, and she returned from her world of inner bliss.

Evan was still inside of her, and still moving, though he now slid in and out in slow deliberate movements.

"Evan, why didn't you . . ."

"We have all night," he answered quickly.

"But . . ."

"I can stop if you want me to," he suggested teasingly.

"Don't stop. Don't ever stop," she said dreamily. She never expected him to take her literally, though.

She lay back and closed her eyes, feeling only Evan's body on top of her, his hard rod inside of her. His steady breathing filled her ears and the sweet smell of his sweat filled her nose. Her body rocked with his as she drifted off.

It seemed like an eternity, and it seemed like a minute, but sometime later Jessie opened her eyes. First she realized how good she felt, then she realized how good Evan felt as he continued to rock her with slow even strokes of his thick shaft. Then with a start she realized the sky was growing lighter.

"Evan . . ."

"Mmmm . . ."

"It's almost dawn."

"It's beautiful, isn't it?"

"That's not what I mean. We have to stop," she said urgently.

"Whatever you want," he said with a sly grin, but he continued to thrust gently on top of her.

"You know I don't really want you to, but people will be getting up soon."

"I'd hate to leave you unsatisfied."

"Evan, I'm anything but."

"Then I guess we should stop now."

"Not just yet," Jessie said seductively. "In a minute." With that Jessie contracted her inner muscles, and Evan let out a surprised moan of ecstasy as her body gripped his manhood.

Jessie squeezed him again and Evan smiled. "I don't know if I can last even a minute if you keep doing that."

"Then don't," she urged him. But her body did more to persuade him than any words spoken from her lips. She continued to flex and grip, and Evan began to pump even faster.

With his increased movements Jessie began to realize just how excited she was, and how close she was to another climax. His endless minutes of soft loving had brought her right to the brink where she had hovered almost since her last release.

"Don't stop, Evan." It was almost a desperate plea.

"I couldn't even if I wanted to." His voice was thick and throaty. "And don't you stop." His was definitely a desperate plea.

As Jessie squeezed again, the increased friction and Evan's little shudder nearly pushed her over the brink.

Amazingly she could feel Evan growing inside her. She could feel his organ twitch. She raised her hips, and arched her back, and suddenly Evan released.

She could feel his organ contract and pump deep inside her. As he flooded her, her own gates opened and a wave of ecstasy washed over her. She had to bury her face into his chest to keep from crying out.

The sun was still a few minutes from rising, but the long, wonderful night had come to an end.

"Jessie?!"

"Over here, Ki," she answered as she walked back to the wagons. "After sitting all night, I needed to stretch my legs. Evan was up early so we took a walk."

"Anything happen?" Ki asked.

Jessie shook her head. "It was a quiet night."

"Good."

"And how do you feel on this new morn?"

"Ready to get started," he said simply.

"And the sooner the better," agreed Evan.

Chapter 6

The sun grew hotter as it climbed higher in the sky, and the air became extremely dry. By midday the heat had reduced the travelers to sullen silence.

After several changes and combinations, Jessie shared a horse with Evan, Yvette rode with Blain, and Richards and Buck each had their own mount. Ki walked along a few steps behind, content to be by himself.

He was lost in his thoughts and didn't realize Blain had stopped his horse and Yvette had slid off until she was standing next to him.

"Mind if I walk along with you?" she asked. "I can get pretty sore sharing a saddle."

"Walking should help," Ki agreed, and she joined in next to him.

At first she didn't speak but soon started a conversation. "You don't seem very pleased by this," she began tentatively.

"I don't mind walking," Ki answered. "Sometimes I've had to walk for days on end."

"I didn't mean walking; I meant everything. If you don't mind me saying, you seem rather disgusted."

Ki smiled. "Does it really show?"

"Not like a wart on the tip of your nose," she said with a pretty smile of her own. "But if you're looking, it's there." She paused momentarily and studied Ki. "You look surprised. Upset that I can peer through that Oriental inscrutability?"

"Do I appear to be inscrutable?" Ki asked. Yvette shrugged coyly. "Apparently I'm not that inscrutable. At least not totally."

"You're not totally Chinese," she said simply. "Actually I'd say Japanese," she corrected herself quickly. "And I'd say only half Japanese at that."

"That's very good," Ki said, honestly impressed.

Yvette accepted the compliment graciously. "Thank you."

"Most people just realize I'm not white. Chinese, if anything. Sometimes Indian."

Yvette shook her head. "Your eyes give it away. And the strong cheekbones."

"You're a good observer."

"I know men," she said matter-of-factly.

"You're also a good judge of mood and character," Ki continued. "I *am* a little disgusted."

Yvette let out a laugh. "And why shouldn't you be? We're a sorry lot."

Ki looked her in the eyes. "I'm beginning to think otherwise," he said softly.

Yvette blushed, then laughed. "It's not often a man makes me blush. In fact I can't think of the last time. I like you, Ki," she said abruptly as she wrapped her arm in his.

"I'll accept that as a compliment," Ki said, without any effort to try to remove her arm.

"You should," she said with a smile. "I don't say that often. At least not with genuine affection."

Ki was about to answer when he saw something out of the corner of his eye. He turned, and there in the distance a column of black smoke trailed up to the sky.

He slipped away from Yvette. "Jessie," he called, then pointed to the horizon as she turned. It was an unnecessary gesture; she saw the smoke for herself.

"That's our wagons," Evan exclaimed as he, too, saw the black soot.

"How do you know?" Richards asked.

"What else could it be?" Buck snapped.

"It could be anything," Richards continued.

Buck laughed scornfully.

"A brush fire, or a mesquite . . ."

"It's the wagons," Evan answered with a finality that no one cared to argue with.

Jessie dropped to the ground and walked over to Ki. Together they drifted away from the others. "What do you make of it?"

"Someone burned those wagons intentionally," he said somberly.

"The question is, who?"

"And why," Ki added.

"We're not going to start that again, are we?" Jessie said with the slightest trace of humor in her eyes.

Ki shook his head. "We look at things differently."

"Only slightly," Jessie interjected.

"Agreed. We approach things differently, Jessie, but the who or the why will no doubt lead us to the same answer."

"Unfortunately we have no way of looking for that answer."

Ki shook his head. "I think the answer is right here."

"Here?"

Ki nodded. "Right under our noses."

"What are you getting at, Ki?"

"Somebody has gone to great lengths to harass this wagon party."

"Yes, if you want to call robbing, stealing, and murder harassment," she said bitingly.

"They didn't plan to kill Stephen."

"That's a great consolation."

Ki ignored her sarcasm. "Remember, he ambushed them."

"He's dead, just the same," Jessie argued.

"I don't disagree, and I'm not condoning his killing. I'm just saying that somebody—"

"The bandits."

"Probably. These bandits have gone to a lot of trouble to get at or find out something."

"Robbing a near-defenseless group of people is not what I would consider going to a lot of trouble."

Ki smiled. "That's exactly my point, Jessie."

She started to disagree, then stopped suddenly. "Maybe I do understand," she began. "Had they been so inclined the bandits could have easily killed them all the first time around."

"I'm sure of it," Ki remarked.

"There were at least six of them, and only Evan and Buck could be relied upon to offer any resistance."

"I wouldn't underestimate Blain," Ki cautioned.

Jessie looked skeptical. "But even so they were out-numbered. They could have killed them then instead of hanging around."

Ki nodded. "We naturally assumed the bandits had taken what they wanted and had gone. But they hadn't."

"So you think they still want something."

"It's a reasonable assumption."

"Something someone here has, or knows of."

Ki nodded.

Jessie looked distressed. "Perhaps Yvette?"

"Could be any of them."

"I meant as a woman. Maybe all they want is—"

"I doubt it, Jessie. They could have killed the men when they had the chance and taken Yvette right then and there. It's unlikely that they only thought of it later."

"But—"

"Rape isn't an afterthought," he continued. "Especially with men like that. If that's what they wanted, they'd have wanted it from the start."

"I suppose you're right."

"I'm not saying that they don't want her. They might very well, though it's not simply to indulge their pleasures."

"So it could be anybody."

"Or all of them."

"Or some of them."

Ki nodded. "Someone here has something secret that the bandits want."

"What?" Jessie pondered aloud.

Ki smiled. "Looks like this time it's not a who or why, but a what."

"In the end I don't think it matters."

"In the end it doesn't."

"I wonder which one it is?"

"Be careful around all of them," Ki warned seriously.

The significance of the burning wagons was not lost on any of the others either. As Blain put it, "Wagons don't spontaneously combust, not even in this heat."

And there was little doubt who was responsible for the fire. As they discussed it, Jessie watched each person closely, looking for a hint as to who it was that was keeping a secret. Each face in turn showed fear and worry, but no individual gave a clue that he or she was the holder of some knowledge that kept ruthless bandits snapping at their heels.

Jessie could also see that each person was eyeing his companion with suspicion and distrust. They no doubt had come to some of the same conclusions that she and Ki had arrived at earlier, but they remained silent, keeping their accusations to themselves.

The one thing they did voice was their ideas on how to face the inevitable. The bandits were coming after them; on that they all agreed.

Richards wanted to run for it. Evan and Blain both explained the futility of attempting to have seven people on four horses outrun a mob of six each on his own horse.

Yvette wondered why they couldn't hide somewhere. Again it was Evan who brought up the difficulties of finding a place to hide in the flat, barren plain. Although he was right, they did consider the option briefly. If the bandits weren't good trackers, perhaps they could lose them. Jessie even suggested they could split up, then double back on their own trail.

It wasn't a bad idea, but Ki rejected it at once. "This isn't the type of terrain that allows you to cover your trail easily," he stated. Then he added, "And if they've tracked them this far, we won't lose the bandits that simply."

Jessie noted keenly that no one thought it odd that Ki had said that they had been tracked by the bandits. Perhaps they all knew more than they were letting on.

Buck was even willing to make a stand right where they were. "I don't see no use in trying to put off what's bound to happen. We can run all day, but they're bound to catch up with us."

Surprisingly, Evan agreed. "This here's as good a place as any."

"I don't agree," Ki said.

"We might as well get it over with quickly," Richards said with a deep sigh.

Evan continued. "We got enough guns to hold them off. We could fort up right here."

"Strategically, it's a poor choice," Ki repeated again. "There's no cover, no safe place to fall back on, and they could come at us from all sides."

"I'm with Ki," Blain announced. "Even with their extra guns"—he gestured to Jessie and Ki—"I think we'd have a tough go of it. We should try for anything that will tip the odds in our favor."

"But you already said that there's no place to hide. . . ." Yvette began.

"We don't need a place to hide," Jessie explained. "An arroyo, a dry gulch, even a thick stand of mesquite . . ."

"I think we can do much better than that," Ki said optimistically. He turned to Evan. "Which way is Little Springs?"

"Thataway, a hair north of due east," he said, pointing.

"Then I think," Ki said, pointing northwest, "we might find an old stage depot in about twenty some-odd miles."

"The Butterfield Overland," Jessie said excitedly. "As I recall, Little Springs was founded right along the old mail route."

"That's where I'll place my money," Blain was the first to say.

"We'll fort up there and hold the bastards off till they pull out or drop," Evan added enthusiastically.

"I think we can make it before before dark," Ki remarked.

"But will it be before they catch up with us?" Yvette asked. It was a question that was on all their minds.

"There's only one way to tell," Jessie said.

"And the sooner we head out, the better our chances,"

finished Blain. "Ki, if you'd like to ride some, I can hoof it awhile."

"I think we should all ride," Jessie said. "Let's push the horses as much as we can. It's important we make that depot."

Ki nodded. "The horses can rest tonight." He assessed the situation quickly, going over the possibilities. Buck was clearly out, the man was too big to double up. The same might be said for Blain. As distasteful as it was, the choice was evident. "I'll ride with Richards," Ki announced.

The bank teller was equally unhappy with the arrangement, though he didn't utter a word of complaint. But before Ki could swing up onto the horse, Blain dismounted. "Here, Ki, I think it'll be better all around if I ride with him."

Ki didn't protest. In fact he rather liked the idea of riding with Yvette in his arms.

What he didn't realize was how much he would like it. At first the fresh sweet smell of gardenia perfume filled his head; then, the more subtle, earthy aroma of her warm hair wafted up to his nostrils. He could feel the heat emanate off her body, and periodically as the horse swayed he would feel the weight of her body pressing against his.

It came as no surprise then that his manhood soon became engorged. Ki tried to shift his position, but there was nowhere to move. As she leaned back Yvette couldn't help but feel Ki's hard erection.

Ki felt the need to apologize. "I hope that doesn't offend you," he began.

"On the contrary, I take it as a compliment."

No further words were necessary. Especially since Yvette now took every opportunity to purposely rub her body against his hard shaft.

But that brought another question to Ki's mind, and though he thought he knew the answer, he wanted to ask anyway. "How well do you know Evan?"

"How well or how intimately? You forget, Ki, I have a keen eye when it comes to sizing up men." Then without waiting for his reply she explained the extent of her relationship with Evan. She then asked about his involvement with Jessie.

After he explained, Yvette leaned back against him. "She must be a very strong-willed woman. I don't think I could resist you for that long."

"Jessie's like a sister to me," Ki said frankly.

Yvette turned her head to him and smiled. "I'm glad you're not my brother."

Three hours later, they stopped to take their bearings. All but Buck dismounted to stretch their legs.

"I'm certain we're in the vicinity," Ki began. "I'm just a little worried that it might be a mile or two north or south of us."

"But I thought you knew where it was," Richards whined.

"I have a good idea," Ki answered, "but with no real landmark to guide us—"

"But I thought you knew this area," the bank teller continued. "How to you expect us to—"

Jessie had heard enough. "Neither Ki nor I have accurate, first-hand knowledge of this region."

"But you said—"

"Shut up, Richards," Evan snapped. "I almost think we should have let him get away that night," he said to no one in particular. "Let him face the bandits alone. See how well he'd fare then."

The fear that others might possibly agree and that he'd be cast off silenced further complaints.

"As I was saying," Jessie continued, "though we've passed through the territory before, we've never wandered this far west. The thing to do is send out scouts. Why don't I ride north, and you go south, Ki."

"I think I better stay here," Ki answered. He still didn't think it was a good idea to leave Buck and Richards alone. For that matter he wondered whether it was wise to leave any of them unattended. "Why don't you go, Evan."

"All right."

Without further ado the two took off in opposite directions. The others had nothing to do but sit and wait.

The wait, however, was not long. Twenty minutes later Jessie returned, shaking her head. "It's not north of us." she said as she dismounted.

"Maybe Evan will have better luck," Yvette said hopefully. She spoke for all of them.

Minutes later Evan came galloping back, waving his arms excitedly. "To the south, about two miles, and maybe about another mile ahead."

"Let's go," Jessie said. They didn't dally.

They came upon it just as the sun was setting. The depot was a one-room adobe building with an adjoining shed for animals. There was a hitching post outside, a water tank shot full of holes, and the bare skeleton of a windmill tower that had long ago been picked clean by scavengers. Shabby and lifeless as the depot was, the group was still glad to find it.

"It's not your hifalutin hotel," Blain remarked as they dismounted. "In fact it looks like it hasn't been inhabited for years."

"It hasn't," Jessie said as she knocked away the cobwebs from the front door. "Not since the war."

"That explains the poor mail service," Evan said with a smile.

Jessie laughed, then explained. "The route was moved north when the conflict broke out. And the company never resumed operations. It's been abandoned ever since."

"Well it has four walls and a roof," Evan noted. "Thick walls," he added as an afterthought.

Blain laughed. "A bath would have been nice, and maybe an after-dinner brandy, but I think I'll do just fine, thank you, with walls that can stop bullets."

Now that they had found shelter, the general mood had improved greatly. Regretfully they ate a cold dinner; Ki didn't think it worth the risk to start a fire. The bandits would probably track them without difficulty, but why announce their location with a telltale trail of smoke?

After the meal, the day's journey took its toll, and everyone was ready to turn in for the night.

"Ki, I'll take the first shift," Jessie offered.

"I don't think there'll be need for that," Ki replied.

"You've walked most of the day," she said sympathetically. "I'd like you to get some sleep tonight."

Ki smiled. "I mean I don't think we'll have to post guards. The bandits won't catch up to us before morning."

Jessie looked at him curiously, but said nothing. The bandits could show up at any moment, and Ki knew that. He had something in mind, and she played along.

"But what's to stop him from trying to run off again?" Buck asked. It was clear who "him" referred to. "I'll stand watch."

Ki shook his head. "If there's going to be any fighting tomorrow, we'll all need clear heads."

"We'll also need our horses," Buck continued, not bothering to hide his contempt of Richards.

"I'll sleep in the shed and keep an eye on the animals," Ki said. With that and a good-night nod to Jessie, Ki left.

For a moment Jessie wondered what Ki was planning. She doubted he would sleep much, though he wanted the others to think he would. Then curiously she realized that Buck had been extremely quiet, until then.

Ki sat cross-legged in the shadows of the adobe wall. His eyes were closed but he wasn't asleep. He was in a light meditative state that would leave him as refreshed as that many hours of sleep. Yet he was wide awake to what was going on around him. In fact, his mind, both calmed and focused, left his senses even more alert to the warning signs of an intruder.

Therefore he was not surprised by the scrape of gravel.

Chapter 7

Ki stood up quickly and silently, flattening himself against the wall. There was the muffled sound of a foot stepping lightly. The noise was coming from around the corner of the building, but the footsteps were heading in his direction.

He inched his way to the edge of the wall and waited. There was another footfall, and Ki prepared to pounce.

The figure turned the corner and Ki lashed out. His body moved automatically. There was no hesitation, no doubt. Speed was essential to mastering the martial arts, but it wasn't simply physical speed. Fast as he was, Ki possessed no superhuman trait that enable him to move that much quicker than another human. There was no physiological difference that distinguished Ki from other men. Ki, though, was substantially faster than those others. It was his mental clarity and concentration that gave him his speed. His mind was totally focused. He knew beforehand what exactly it was he planned to do. His brain never had to falter; his body never received a mixed message. His muscles would swiftly and expediently do their job. This time the command was a *tegatana-uchi* to the *atemi* point below the ear.

But it was the same focused concentration and mental agility that allowed him, in mid-strike, to alter his plan. Whether it was the faint aroma of gardenia that he smelled, or the feminine silhouette that he saw, his brain sent an urgent message to his body.

In mid-air his muscles froze. Instead of a temporarily paralyzing blow to the neck, his hand opened and softened to grab the shoulder harmlessly. There was still some force behind it, and Ki's other hand shot around to the mouth to muffle the faint scream of pain and surprise that he knew would follow.

"It's all right," Ki said softly.

"You nearly scared me half to death," Yvette whispered, after a startled cry. "You also nearly knocked me cold," she said as she rubbed her neck.

"I wasn't expecting you," Ki said simply. He began to massage her neck with his strong fingers. "You'll have a little bruise there, but the pain should fade quickly."

"It's all right. I just wasn't expecting it."

"That makes two of us," Ki said with a smile.

"I couldn't sleep in there," she said by way of an explanation. "Too stuffy."

"It's nicer out here," Ki agreed.

Yvette looked him in the eye, and smiled. "Truth is, I couldn't help thinking about you."

Ki took her in his arms and pulled her close. She parted her lips and offered them to him. They kissed deeply and passionately.

Her breasts, pointed and soft, rubbed against his chest as she leaned against him. Slowly she began to gyrate her hips, and she moaned softly as she felt his manhood stiffen. Her hands strayed down his body, then up his leg. "I kept thinking of you, so firm and hard."

"I've been thinking of you, too." Ki admitted.

"Then you don't mind that I came out to be with you?"

"I was hoping you might." That was one of the reasons he wanted to sleep outside. That was not the only reason, but he didn't tell her that.

Yvette smiled and and they kissed again.

"Ki, there's something I want to tell you," she began as she pulled away.

"Shhh."

"No, it's important—"

"Quiet!" he commanded.

At first she had misunderstood, and thought that he wasn't interested in hearing any explanation she wanted to give, but now she realized it was something different.

"Don't move," he whispered in her ear.

Yvette was still. She could see Ki listening closely, but she couldn't hear anything herself.

"Was everyone asleep when you came out here?" Ki asked.

She nodded. "I'm pretty sure I didn't wake anyone."

"Stay here," Ki instructed. "Count to five, then walk quickly but quietly back inside."

"What's wrong?" Her voice was straining not to show her fear.

"I don't know," Ki answered. "But if I'm not back in five minutes, wake Jessie."

Yvette nodded. Then a question came to mind. "What should I tell her?"

"That you heard something outside. Now remember—count to five, slowly, then get inside."

He turned and silently made his way around to the shed. He stood a moment, listening again. Then he heard it out in the distance. A man crawling steadily forward.

He slipped a *shuriken* into his hand and backed up along the wall. With the corner of the building between him and the intruder he veered off into the night. He was hoping to outflank the man and come up behind him.

Ki realized there was a certain amount of risk involved. Once he left the protective shadows of the depot, he was exposed and vulnerable. But he wanted to try and overtake the man before he closed in on the building.

Ki looked up. The moon was bright and there were few clouds. But the situation was not hopeless. The man would have his eyes trained on the building. If Ki swung a wide loop he would be out of the man's field of vision. In addition, when crawling, most men tended to keep their noses close to the ground. With a little luck Ki would pounce on the unsuspecting man the way an eagle swoops down on a snake.

He moved swiftly, flowing naturally like the wind. He had a certain animal grace, a *ninja*-trained ability to move and not be spotted. But of course that would work only within certain limits.

Unfortunately Ki was about to exceed those limits.

He had completed enough of an arc and was about to come upon the man from behind when he heard a warning shout come from his left. Then there was the sharp crack of a gunshot.

Ki dove headlong into the dirt. As he did so he heard a second shot come from in front of him. Luck, at least, was still with him. The shout, though it had not been meant for him, had saved his life.

There were two men out there. The one he was stalking, and another one that he had not been aware of, farther to the left. It was that second man who had spotted him, and fearing his companion was in danger, had issued the warning.

Ki was in a tight fix. He had lost the element of surprise and was caught out in the open facing two men, both

70

armed with guns. With his location known the light of the moon became a crucial factor. He couldn't risk exposing himself even for a moment.

He was just planning his next move when a volley of rifle fire exploded from the adobe depot.

Ki didn't waste any more time in thought. He sprang to his feet and raced to the building, dodging every few steps, weaving in and out as he ran. Ki kept his head low as the gunshots from the building continued. In no time at all he was diving through the opened wood door.

"You all right, Ki?" Jessie asked immediately.

He nodded as he picked himself up off the floor. "Thanks to you."

"I just supplied the cover," she said with a modest smile. "You had the hard part. You had to make the dash in."

"Well it was a lot simpler, thanks to you."

Had they been alone Jessie would have teased him a little more about it. Perhaps questioning if he was losing his ability to dodge unfriendly bullets. But they were not alone, and this was not the time nor the place for playful banter.

"What's going on?" Blain wondered aloud. "Who's out there?" As soon as he asked it he realized he didn't need an answer. It was all too obvious. "But I thought you said they wouldn't be here till morning."

A shrug was all the answer Ki gave.

"That really doesn't matter," Evan remarked. "The question is, what are we going to do now?"

"That's entirely up to them," Jessie said as she tilted her head towards the window.

"They won't attack, will they?" Richards asked.

"We can't say, can we?" Jessie said patiently. "We'll have to stay alert."

71

"They'll be somebody to stand guard, won't there?" Richard continued.

"We'll put someone at each window."

The back wall was solid; the two sides each had a window, and the front had two.

"We can get by with three," Ki suggested. "One to a side."

"That means you won't have to worry, Richards," Buck snapped. "You can just sit there and guard your money."

The teller turned away, clearly embarrassed, not by the insult, but by open reference to his cache of money.

Jessie continued. "I'll take this side."

"I'll take the other," Evan said.

"The front's mine," Buck said unceremoniously.

"The rest of you can try and get some sleep," Jessie began.

Blain laughed. "I don't think I'll get much sleep. But not because you don't make me feel protected," he added with a polite smile. "I'll watch the other front window."

"Can I do anything?" Yvette asked.

"You may have to, but I hope not," Jessie answered. Yvette looked insulted, and Jessie clarified. "You can tend to any injuries."

"I see what you mean," Yvette said solemnly. "But at least I've done it before."

"Good."

"Looks like we're all set, then," Evan said as he cracked open his window shutter. "We got all sides covered."

Blain had a last question. "What's to stop them from coming up on our backs?"

"Me," Ki replied as he reached down and picked up Jessie's saddle rifle. "I'll be on the roof."

Ki was pretty sure any attack would come from the rear. After facing the heavy gunfire that had kept the two bandits pinned down, Ki doubted they would try and mass a frontal assault.

It was important then that someone trustworthy and competent be stationed up on the roof. There wasn't much of a choice. Ki was beginning to trust Evan, and for that reason wanted to keep the man with Jessie. Especially when he himself couldn't be there.

Ki lay flat against the roof, one eye always searching the distance. Now the bright moonlight was to his advantage; any movements the bandits were to make would be plainly visible.

Ki felt it very important to keep a sharp lookout. He wanted to keep the bandits as far away as possible. That meant spotting their first moves and keeping them pinned down before they advanced very far. That was essential, not because their safety depended upon it; the walls were thick and there was enough firepower in the building to repel an attack, at least initially. Ki was thinking farther on down the road.

Until now, there had been only one fatality. And in a sense that was not part of the bandits' plan. It was not a deliberate premeditative murder. As long as more men didn't get killed, Ki felt there might be a way to talk themselves out of this situation. The bandits might be willing to strike a bargain. But once one of the bandits got killed, Ki didn't expect reason and logic to prevail. There would be angry, hot tempers that would be cooled by only one thing —bloodshed.

For that reason, Ki didn't want to let any of the bandits get close enough to the building to risk getting shot.

For a moment he considered telling the men below not

to aim to kill, but he discarded the notion. They no doubt felt their lives were being threatened. A scared, cornered man is not going to aim down the sight of a gun and try to maim his would-be killer. No amount of reasoning or logic could convince them to do that. There was also the simple question of marksmanship; could Blain and Evan aim accurately enough to just wound? Ki doubted it. Buck was not unfamiliar with guns, and he might have the required skill, but the man's temperament made it unlikely that he would do anything but aim to kill.

All in all, Ki figured the best chance lay with him, and the rifle. A good marksman should be able to keep the rushers at bay. Over the long haul the only problem would be bullets. Ki wondered if he had enough for a sustained assault. He had two pockets full of cartridges. That should be enough. He started to do some mental calculations then stopped.

Bullets or no bullets, in the long run, the bandits had a very definite advantage. Ki only hoped it wouldn't come down to that.

The rush came in the dark-gray moments before dawn. The moon was not shining, and the sunrise was still a long way off. The landscape was a bleak, colorless plain, which made everything—rock, plant, and man—blend into one. The approaching morning provided better cover than the moonlit night.

Ki's first rifle shot came as a surprise; the dirt the bullet kicked up was an even bigger surprise. Coming up on the blind side, the bandits did not expect to be spotted. Though there was some doubt on their part, Ki observed with a wry smile. Had they thought it totally safe they would have walked right up to the rear wall. Instead they crouched and moved with care. The caution proved warranted, and the bandits went sprawling forward.

From his higher elevation Ki could see their every movement, and every time they raised a head Ki squeezed on the rifle trigger and sent dirt flying into their faces.

They started lifting their guns and firing blindly, and Ki let them. There was little chance of them hitting anything, and Ki didn't mind watching them waste their bullets. Apparently the bandits also realized the futility of it, and stopped.

For a few minutes there was a restless pause while the bandits reconsidered.

"What's going on, Ki"? Evan called up. "Everything all right?"

"They tried coming up from behind," Ki answered in a low but clear voice. "They didn't get very far."

"How many did you get?"

"None."

Evan was silent, and Ki could feel the man's disappointment. "Well, at least we put the fear of God in them," he said at last.

"There were only three of them," Ki continued. "I think the others were waiting to attack the front. Be prepared."

"I'll tell Buck," Evan answered.

Ki decided to heed his own advice, and shifted position so he could keep an eye on the front as well. Evan's words reminded Ki that Buck was guarding that direction. That made it all the more important for Ki to stop the attackers before they came within range of Buck's handgun.

It was a good thing Ki moved; he saw two men crawling forward. He raised the rifle, aimed, and fired. They hugged the ground.

Ki quickly turned around in time to catch the three men advancing on the rear. He fired hastily. His shots were poorly aimed, but it didn't matter. He had already proven his ability, and the bandits were not going to press their luck. Again, for a few moments, things were calm.

But Ki doubted they would stay that way. In a few minutes the bandits moved again. Ki found by firing two shots in one direction, then rolling on his side to fire another few shots in the other direction it would appear that there were two men on the roof. His ruse and his marksmanship proved effective, and the bandits gained only a few feet.

As their companions in the rear had tried, the bandits in the front raised their guns and tried to fire blindly. This time, though, their shots were answered by the gunfire from within the building. Ki didn't bother to respond and instead kept his eyes on the men sneaking up on the back. They tried to move but got nowhere.

"Save your fire; they're way out of reach," Ki heard Jessie order.

"Then what's the point of keeping them at a distance?" he heard Blain ask. "Why not let the varmints move in so we can cut 'em down, once and for all?"

Ki was afraid someone would suggest that. He was interested in hearing Jessie's response.

She thought a moment before answering. "It works both ways," she began. "Right now they can't shoot us, either. But bullets travel in two directions."

Blain didn't answer; no one did.

The sky was getting brighter, and the sun would be up in a few minutes. Ki saw the men in the rear retreat. They backed up cautiously; then, when they were out of range of the rifle, they got up and walked away.

Though the surrounding area appeared flat, the stage depot was really in the middle of a shallow basin. After a couple hundred yards, Ki lost sight of the men as they topped the shallow ridge.

At the front, Ki saw the bandits there retreating as well. He watched them till they too were out of sight; then he dropped down to the ground.

He didn't expect the bandits to return for a while, but when they did, they would no doubt return in force. They would also have a plan, and might not be discouraged so easily.

What was it they wanted? Ki wondered again. Was it worth risking their lives for? If the answer was yes, there were tough times ahead.

Chapter 8

They took turns sleeping throughout the day. But at all times they kept a lookout up on the roof. Ki no longer cared if the guard was a capable marksman. It was only necessary for the lookout to wake Ki in the event of any impending activity.

But the call to action never came. The time passed slowly, and by midday everyone was growing tense and restless.

"Maybe they've gone," Richards was the first to say. "Maybe they just picked up and left."

Surprisingly, no one ridiculed the idea. "It's possible," Evan agreed.

"They can't get to us," Blain remarked. "So maybe they did throw in their cards. No sense hanging around in the middle of God-knows-where—at least not in this heat," he added as he wiped his sweaty brow with a white handkerchief.

On the whole they seemed pretty optimistic, but there

79

was something essential that had escaped the three men. Ki wondered whether he should inform them of the one important aspect they were overlooking. He decided, since no one had asked his opinion, to keep the information to himself.

"Maybe we should pull up stakes ourselves," Evan suggested. "Get, while the getting's good."

"And what happens once we get out there?" Yvette asked. She got puzzled looks but no answers. "We don't know that they've gone. They could be waiting for us, just over the next rise."

"Or they could be halfway to a saloon by now," Blain countered.

"I reckon we won't know till we step out there," Evan said almost to himself.

Richards was once again looking worried. "We can't take that chance."

"I'm beginning to wonder about that," Blain began. "We did pretty good for ourselves right here. Maybe I was wrong before. Maybe we do have a better'n even chance."

"But would you risk your life on that?" the bank teller asked.

"I don't think it's my life you're so concerned with, Mr. Richards," Blain snapped. "And, yes, pretty soon we may have to stick our necks out there."

"If they're gone it ain't too much of a risk, now is it?" Richards fired back. "And if they ain't, I see no reason why we can't fight them off from in here."

It was clear to Jessie they were going around in circles. "The fact of the matter is, we don't know where the bandits are," she said sternly.

"Then we'll have to find out," Evan said resolutely. "Maybe send out a scout or two."

"And we'll find them like your pal, Stephen," Blain argued.

"Not necessarily."

"There'll be six against one."

"I ain't saying one man should go up against the bandits, just scout around and see if he can spot 'em."

"And what if the bandits spot him first?" Blain said snidely.

Evan started to answer, but then fell silent.

Blain drove home his point. "And who would you send? Ask for volunteers? How 'bout you, Richards? Would you go? Don't even answer," he said with disgust. "I wouldn't trust you to come back." He looked to Evan. "I wouldn't send a man out to get killed, and I wouldn't trust a man to come back if he weren't."

"I say they're gone," Richards repeated firmly, trying to make up for his loss of face.

"Shut up," Blain snapped.

"I'm willing to try," Richards stated.

Blain crossed to the door and opened it. "Then go. . . ."

"This isn't solving anything," Jessie said loudly. "Snarling at each other isn't going to help."

"What choice do we have?" Blain asked rather foolishly.

"We have one—we wait," she answered.

Jessie caught sight of Ki's face. His seemingly deadpan expression told her much. The worst possible thing to do was to wait it out, they both knew that. But Jessie suspected this was what Ki wanted. As the tension increased, something was bound to snap. Would the person with the most to lose crack first? Or would peer pressure expose the secret?

Either way, it was vital to know what the bandits wanted. Since they couldn't just ride out and ask them, the answer had to come from within this room. Jessie looked over the assortment of people. It was curious that Yvette had been the most level-headed. She was not willing to rush headlong into the waiting arms of the bandits. Was she the one with something to hide, or was she, as a woman, able to separate her own ego, and see the situation clearly? She didn't have to prove she was brave; she didn't have to worry about showing fear. She had no reputation to uphold. Did that aid in her perception? Or was it that she knew that the bandits wouldn't leave until they got what they came for? Jessie couldn't answer that.

And what about Richards? The man was scared, but he was the type that would always show fear in a tight spot. Did he have a good reason to be that worried, or was he simply a weakling? Was it just the question of the money he carried, or was there more?

Then Blain. Blain, Jessie noted, was looking much less dapper than at their first meeting. Though he was clearly used to the finer things in life, the man was not soft. Yet he was the first to show strain. As the gentleman gambler Jessie took him to be—his constant reference to cards and odds had led her to that conclusion—that seemed unusual. But then again, maybe not. A good gambler is well aware of the odds, and makes his bets accordingly. This was a situation clearly beyond the gaming table. Blain had no inside line on the odds. Things were out of his control. And a good gambler never lets things get out of his control. Had he miscalculated? Did he make a play for the pot and come up short? Had he gambled and lost? Or, more importantly, had he won? For every winner there's a loser, and the bigger the win the harder the loss. Were those bandits nothing but sore losers out to even the score?

Then she turned to Evan. She tried to look at him critically, but she found it difficult. They had made love last night. They had shared their bodies under the stars. They had been open and intimate with each other. But that didn't mean he couldn't have a secret. He had told her things about himself, but what didn't he tell her? Actually, now that she thought about it, his most recent past was glossed over. Was that because there was something to hide? Something that would have the bandits following him?

Jessie couldn't answer. She couldn't answer any of these questions. Then she looked into Evan's eyes, and she softened. She didn't want to go on intuition alone, but hers told her Evan was not the cause of the problem. But she could always be wrong. Though her feelings rarely erred, there was bound to be a first time.

Evan caught her staring at him and his eyes lit up as his face stretched into a grin. Jessie then recalled a bit of Ki's advice. "There's not a snake under every rock, but if you look long enough you're bound to find one," he had said once when she was looking hard for an answer. Perhaps she was doing that now, too. Except someone here was hiding something. Then she smiled to herself; come to think of it, she had been right that last time too.

The gunshot snapped her from her thoughts. She rushed to the door but Ki had beaten her to it. "See anything?" he shouted up to Buck.

"There's something out there," he answered from atop the roof.

"I can't see anything," Ki replied.

"Well, they're out there just the same," Buck growled.

Ki grabbed hold of the wooden beam that extended out from the roof and swung himself up. Still he saw nothing. "Probably just wanting to know if we were awake," Ki said amiably.

"Well we're more'n awake," Buck answered and climbed down. "I've done my time up there," he said and walked into the cool, dark adobe room.

Jessie watched him go. She was sorry he had not been in the room for their earlier discussion. She would have been interested in seeing his reaction. To put it mildly, Buck kept his cards close to his chest. It wasn't odd for a drifter to keep silent, but Buck's odd mixture of truculence and contempt made her think twice about his silence. It was one thing to keep your opinions to yourself, but Jessie wondered if he was keeping more than his opinions private. Jessie thought a moment, trying to figure out his game. People who played their cards close to their chest usually had an ace hiding somewhere. He demanded close watching. She would keep a close eye on Buck, just like she would keep a close watch on all the others.

Evan climbed up to the roof to join Ki. "You believe Buck really saw something?" he asked softly.

"I don't know," Ki answered honestly. "But I don't think it matters."

"Why not?" Evan said curiously.

He studied the man. Though Ki was not inclined to trust strangers, neither did he distrust them. And he couldn't help but notice the mutual attraction between Evan and Jessie. Ki decided there would be no harm in speaking openly. At worst he would only be fueling the fire, and that didn't seem so bad anyway.

"After sticking around these past days, and trailing you here, I don't think they'd leave just because we've shot up a little dirt in their faces."

Evan laughed. "Put that way it makes a lot of sense. Why didn't you say that inside?"

"No one asked me," Ki said simply.

Evan gave him a sidelong glance. "You're an interesting fellow, Ki. And I'm damned glad you're here."

"I'm not so sure everyone feels that way. Some might think quite the opposite."

"You don't strike me as a man who cares much what others think," Evan said seriously. Then he changed the subject. "I can stand guard awhile if you'd like."

"All right," Ki agreed, then dropped down to the ground.

• • •

The shooting began at twilight. When it started it was almost a welcome relief. The hours of nervous waiting had come to an end, and now activity, even dangerous and perhaps deadly activity, was a refreshing change.

Blain was stationed on the roof, and as soon as he spotted the bandits, Ki went up to join him.

Though the bandits seemed more determined, Ki noted that they were definitely taking fewer risks. There were more of them, and they centered their attack on the front of the building. More shots were fired, from both sides, but the bandits didn't press for the advantage. Ki thought he understood why; and he didn't like it.

Little was accomplished by either side, and by nightfall the bandits had retreated.

The night progressed as slowly as the day, and was in its own right even more nerve-wracking. There had been sporadic incidents throughout the night. None of them could be construed as a major assault; in fact, after only a quick exchange of gunfire things would quiet down until the next incident, twenty minutes, forty minutes, or an hour, later.

Shortly after the moon had risen, Ki had made what seemed like a daring decision; he dispensed with the rooftop lookout. They hadn't spotted a man trying to sneak up from the rear since yesterday, and Ki doubted they would. It was easier to change shifts without having to send a man to the roof, and as Ki explained, a lot safer.

Though there was some apprehension at first to the elimination of the guard, Ki's last point—safety—went over easy. No one fancied having his ass shot as he tried to climb up to the roof.

But it was a short-lived relief. The pressure was building in all of them, but Richards was the one that let it out first. "What are they doing out there?" he nearly exploded.

"Why don't they rush us once and for all and get it over with?"

"Time is on their side," Ki said bluntly.

"But what's the point of all this?" the bank teller whined. "What do they expect to accomplish?"

"I think they're doing just what they set out to do," Ki replied.

Blain let out a dry laugh. "They're staying awake just like us. I can't see the point in that, either."

Ki almost smiled. "First, I'm sure only one man is awake at a time. The others have no problem sleeping. They're not holed up worrying about when the real attack might come."

"I'm beginning to see," Blain muttered.

"And secondly, by morning we'll be so tight we'll jump at anything."

"That's it, you're right," Evan said with sudden realization.

Ki nodded.

"We'll be nervous, bleary-eyed wrecks, come morning."

Again Ki nodded.

"Then knowing that, we should try to get some sleep ourselves, or at least try to relax," Evan concluded.

"I plan to do just that," Ki said as he leaned back against the wall and closed his eyes.

His eyes weren't closed long when he heard Evan's voice speaking softly. "Why are they doing this?" he asked nobody in particular.

Richards chose to answer. "Because those bastards want us dead, that's why."

"If that was true they could have killed us days ago, when they first robbed us," Evan countered.

Richards erupted. "How do I know why they're doing

this? Why ask me? Ask him, or her. I don't know anything."

It sounded to Ki like it was just the opposite—a disclaimer made by someone who knew quite a lot but didn't want to tell. He opened his eyes.

"Calm down," Evan said rather harshly. "I wasn't asking you anything. I was just wondering, that's all."

"Well don't wonder and look at me," Richards said nervously.

"Why not?" Buck's voice was a low growl.

"Because I don't know anything about those bandits. I don't know why the hell they're after us."

"I wouldn't say that," Buck said meanly.

"I tell you, I don't know why," Richards almost shrieked.

"I do," Ki said softly. All eyes turned to him. "They're after you because one of you has something they want."

"They took everything," Blain said quickly. "What more could they want?"

Ki shrugged. "We'll find out in due time," he said calmly and again closed his eyes. Ki hadn't taken two breaths before Richards was again speaking.

"I know what you're all thinking. And it's not true. They don't know about my money. They don't know a thing about it," he raved. "If they did, why didn't they take it when they first had the chance?"

Ki had to admit it was a good question. A question he didn't have an answer for. There were a lot of answers he didn't have, at least not at this point. But that didn't bother him; sometimes it was just as important to be asking the right questions. Untroubled, he closed his eyes.

Buck's harsh voice brought Ki out of his light sleep. "Where you goin'?" Buck was asking.

"To relieve myself," Richards answered.

"Need yer pack to do that?"

"I ain't going to leave it here for the likes of you. . . ."

"You saying what I think you are?" Buck's words were an unmasked challenge.

"I'm just saying that I'm going out and I'm taking my bag with me."

"And I say you ain't."

The others were watching with interest, but were refusing to get involved. After all, Richards had already tried to run out on them once; who knew if he would try it again?

"How you going to stop me?" Richards asked.

Buck didn't answer; he only smiled. That in itself was enough.

"You going to shoot me right here just because I gotta step outside for a minute." The bank teller tried to sound calm, but it was clear it was a struggle. He appealed to the others. "You all going to stand by and let him?"

"There ain't no love lost between us, friend," Blain said coldly. "Leave that pack here and we know you're coming back."

"I leave it here and I'll never see my money again," he accused.

"What are you saying?" Buck said threateningly.

Richards stood his ground. "You know exactly what I'm saying. You're as bad as they are," he said, tilting his head to the door. "Least they don't keep no pretense 'bout it."

"I don't like what I'm hearing," Buck said with a mean smile.

"Maybe 'cause it's the truth."

"I've heard enough," Buck said as he started to move towards the frightened teller.

"All I wanted to do was step outside a minute." Richards spoke rapidly. "I won't leave my pack here, 'cause it won't be safe. I'll never see my money again. But if you're afraid I'll take off, one of you can come out with me."

"Seems fair enough," Buck said as his lips stretched into a thin smile. "Let's go."

Richards almost panicked. "Not you."

"Why not?"

"I'm no fool," he said looking to the others. "I go out with him and I'll wind up with a bullet in my back—"

Buck moved quickly. Richards never saw the backhand that smashed into his cheek and knocked him over.

But Blain and Evan did, and both men rushed to pull Buck off the defenseless Richards. It was a bit of a struggle, but they managed it. Buck calmed down, and Evan and Blain released him. Buck gave them each a dirty look but said nothing. He turned his attention back to Richards, who was picking himself up and wiping blood from the corner of his mouth.

"This don't change nothing," Buck said flatly. "You ain't going less I go with you."

"I'll go with him," Ki announced loudly.

Buck turned angrily to Ki, but before he could say anything Blain spoke. "Sounds fair to me."

Buck started to protest but Blain cut him off. "I think we can trust Ki," he said simply. "That all right with you, Richards?"

The teller nodded.

Richards took care of business, then turned to go back inside. Ki stopped him.

"I think it might be best if you left the bag out here." Richards looked horrified by the idea, and Ki quickly continued. "Hide it. Put it somewhere where it will be safe."

"I'm not letting it out of my sight," Richards said as he clung tightly to the pack.

"I don't think that's the best place for it. We stopped Buck this time, but next time . . ."

"You're just trying to get it away from me," the teller accused.

"I'm trying to help."

"You're as bad as the rest."

"I'm trying to keep you from getting hurt," Ki continued.

"You just want my money, but you can't have it. I won't let you—"

Richards was still raving when Ki's foot smashed into his side. The bank teller doubled over, holding his ribs. Ki stepped forward and snatched the bag off his shoulder. The bank teller glared at Ki, but was helpless to stop him.

"If I wanted your money, that's all I'd have to do," Ki said plainly, then he tossed the bag back to Richards. "When Buck decides he wants it bad enough he'll do something similar. But he may leave you with something more permanent than a bruised rib."

"He can't shoot me, not with everyone watching. I can't believe you'd let him get away with that," Richards continued to argue.

"We won't always be around to stop him," Ki started to say, then changed his mind. "It's your money, Richards," he said with a shrug, then started towards the building.

"Wait . . ."

Buck noticed immediately. "Where's the pack?" he demanded suspiciously.

"I hid it. Put it someplace safe. . . ."

Buck's eyes raged with fury. His mouth twisted into an ugly snarl.

"You'll never get your hands on it," Richards taunted.

"You dirty double-crosser," Buck said angrily as he

reached for his gun. It came out of his holster in one smooth motion. He ignored the teller completely and pointed his colt directly at Ki.

"I warned you," Buck hissed.

Chapter 9

"Drop it, Buck!" Evan ordered. Evan wasn't fast with a gun; he never would have beaten Buck in a draw, but he didn't have to. He was standing behind Buck, and he had his rifle leveled on the man's broad back.

Buck didn't turn around. He stood there, looking as if he were considering the alternatives.

"Do it!" It was Blain, and he too had his gun out. "There's no reason to be getting that way" he said softly.

Jessie let out her breath and slipped her own gun back into its holster. No one had seen her draw, but in fact, hers had been the first gun out. It now seemed unnecessary, and she put it away before anyone noticed.

Without a word of apology Buck lowered his gun. "I need some air," he said and started for the door.

"He's going out to look for my money," Richards complained.

"Shut up," Evan snapped. "Easy, Buck, don't get riled up. It's just foolish talk."

Buck, ignoring them both, stepped through the door.

"You'd think we'd have enough problems without creating any more," Yvette said aloud.

Evan agreed. "We're sure acting like we're our own worst enemy. . . ."

"Well at least some of this is settled," Blain said. "Maybe it will start getting better."

"It will just get worse," Ki said dryly.

"As long as we keep those two apart . . ."

"We still have the bandits to contend with," Ki reminded them.

"I thought we were doing all right," Evan said.

"And the longer we hold them off, the . . ." Blain trailed off.

"Every day works to their advantage," Ki said firmly. "We're already running out of water," he said seriously.

"I never thought about that," Blain admitted.

"I'm sure they have," Ki said. "They can afford to sit out there day after day."

"But they'll need water, too."

"There's nothing to stop one of them from riding to the nearest watering hole to refill their canteens, while the rest keep an eye on us."

"If they can do it, why can't we?" Evan said. "In the middle of the night one of us should be able to sneak out."

"To where?" Ki asked. "Do you know where there's water? We'll just have to sit tight and see what develops. We should have enough water, if we're careful, to last another day."

The information did not please any of them. The realization that they could very well be at the mercy of the bandits created a dark mood, and the conversation abruptly ended. No one noticed when Buck returned a few minutes later.

No one seemed to notice when Ki stepped out either.

94

However, Blain did notice when Jessie got up and walked outside. A quick study of the room showed Ki was also missing. He had a tough moment of indecision; then, in a show of mental strength and determination, he made up his mind.

Jessie caught up to Ki at the animal shed. "Things certainly are moving along," Jessie remarked.

"Perhaps," Ki answered.

"Someone in the bunch is soon going to be bawling like a calf without its mother."

"As our friend Blain would say, it seems like a good bet."

"You don't seem excited by that. . . ."

Ki shrugged. "It no longer seems that important to find out who is the cause of all this and why."

Jessie smiled. "Sounds like you're losing your patience."

Again Ki shrugged. "I can't recall what it's like to be without patience. Is this the feeling?" he asked teasingly.

"This whole experience might be worth it all just to see you impatient."

"I've been impatient before," he retorted.

"I can't recall."

"You just can't tell."

"If I couldn't tell, it's because you didn't show it, and if you didn't show it, it's because you had sufficient control over your emotions," she began to explain. "Which sheds sufficient doubt on whether or not you were truly impatient."

Ki cut her short. "I still am in perfect control."

"A little crotchety."

"I don't think so," he said as he shook his head.

"Then why the comment about no longer caring who has a secret?"

"We've been assuming that if we knew the secret, we would know how to proceed."

Jessie nodded. "We would at least be aware of what this is all about."

"By possessing this knowledge it would give us an advantage," Ki continued, and again Jessie nodded in agreement. "But no matter what, we've made one small error."

"Which is?"

"We're virtually in a state of siege. The bandits are in total control. Whether we know what they want, or who they want, or why, they still call all the shots, and we have to deal with that. Up till now I've been avoiding it."

"What made you change your mind?"

"I'd been too intent upon discovering who was hiding something from us."

"You were certainly creating an interesting situation. And, I might add, it looked like it was working."

"Yes, but I overlooked two things." Jessie raised her eyebrows, and Ki continued. "First, the volatility of the group. In a few more hours they could be shooting at each other. Despite which one was keeping a secret, they were all close to the edge."

"In part because of the tensions you helped to create," Jessie added.

"True, but then I realized that our lack of water was a very real problem, and one I didn't create."

"And now that you've realized all this . . . ?"

"It's a classic military tableau."

"Is it?"

Ki nodded. "The castle under siege. There are many ways to deal with it."

"That's good to know."

"Most of which are unsuccessful."

Oh. I hope you know which are which."

"I was a good student," Ki said seriously.

"This is not a military exercise out of the pages of history, Ki."

"But it is very much like the siege of Osaka Castle in the late fifteenth century."

"How did that turn out?" Jessie wondered.

"The castle was burned to the ground. The defending army died, to a man."

"I see. But this isn't Osaka, or the fifteenth century."

"No."

"So as long as we don't make the same mistakes..." she suggested with a smile.

"Jessie, in a military campaign no one willingly chooses a course of action doomed to failure."

"But they fail, nonetheless."

"At the time, they aren't aware of the outcome," Ki said simply.

"But we have the benefit of their experiences, Ki."

"Spoken like a true student of history," he said with a smile.

"And...?"

"And I don't intend to make the same mistakes others have made."

"Could you be more specific, Ki?"

"I could"—his eyes twinkled—"if I knew what it was I planned to do."

"Ki, I don't believe for one minute you don't have something planned. This is, as you were so quick to point out, a standard military situation. And you being a military strategist...

"Jessie, as you were so quick to point out, this isn't the fifteenth century. And this isn't a simple tactical exercise...."

"Which all the more leads me to believe that you know exactly what you were going to do but won't tell me, either because it's too dangerous and I won't want to do it, or because I'll want to come with you. Or both," she added sternly.

"Precisely."

"Ki . . . !" she exclaimed in frustration.

"What do *you* suggest we do?" Ki asked her.

"You're not changing the subject," she admonished.

"I'm not," he agreed. "Given the circumstance, what do you think we should do?" he repeated.

"In fact, I did come out here to discuss an idea with you," she began. Ki waited expectantly and Jessie proceeded. "I had always thought the key to the situation lay in discovering what it was the bandits wanted."

"For a while that was so," Ki agreed. "It might still be."

"And since we couldn't ask the bandits what it is they were after, we'd have to discover what they wanted ourselves—from the person who had it. But now I'm not so sure."

Ki nodded. "It's become less important."

"Maybe; I don't know." she said with a shrug. "But at this point we can't say."

"All right," Ki conceded.

"Then I realized," Jessie continued excitedly, "why can't we go to the bandits? Why can't we approach them and find out what they want?"

Ki was thinking that over. "It might answer some questions, but—"

"We could do it," she said firmly. "And don't tell me it would be dangerous."

"It would be."

"And so are half the other things we set out to do."

"That doesn't make me like this any more," Ki said seriously.

"It makes more sense than watching that bunch inside take pot shots at each other."

"True."

"Then I don't see why you're against it."

"My only objection is that I don't see the point to it. What purpose would it serve?"

"Ki . . ." she started to protest.

"Listen, Jessie, no matter what it is they want, you know it's not going to be to anyone's benefit but their own. And whatever it is they want, I'm sure it doesn't rightfully belong to them."

"That doesn't surprise me," she answered sarcastically.

"Then regardless of what they want, you won't give it to them." Jessie started to protest but Ki continued. "Since you've taken on these people and their problems, I doubt you'll sell them out. Even our likable Mr. Richards."

"Or the charming Buck," Jessie added. "I suppose you are right, Ki. I won't give in to the bandits, any sooner than I've given in to anybody who thinks he can just take what he wants."

"And what if it happens to belong to them?" Blain said as he approached. "Excuse me for interrupting, but I couldn't help but hear."

"That's all right," Jessie told him. "It's nothing that I wouldn't repeat in front of you."

"I appreciate that, Jessie." Blain said with a polite bow. "An' I appreciate everything you've both done to help us. Which is why I felt the need to come out here and have a word with you."

Jessie and Ki exchanged looks. "Go ahead," Ki encouraged. "Whatever you say won't go beyond us."

Blain nodded and began. "I reckon it won't come as much of a surprise, but I make my living at the gaming tables."

Jessie nodded. "We figured as much. But we don't have any problem with the fact that you're a professional gambler."

"Then you know," he continued with an embarrassed

99

smile, "that we don't always, as a profession—how should I phrase it?—offer the same odds that one would find at a, ah, friendly game."

"We know how gamblers operate," Jessie said flatly, neither condemning nor condoning his actions.

"Then you can understand how it is that I earned some money that others feel isn't rightfully mine." He waited a moment for his words to sink in.

"You're saying you cheating somebody out of his money," Jessie began.

Blain flinched at her choice of words. "I wouldn't exactly put it that way."

"Then how would you put it?" Jessie pressed.

"Card playing is a game of skill, even among professionals. A few nights ago some roustabouts came in looking for an easy mark. They possessed some degree of skill."

"I assume you mean other than an honest sense of the odds," Jessie interjected.

Blain nodded. "Put frankly, they were cheats. They didn't have an honest game going. One would shill for the other, and the deal always went a certain way. But like I said, even crooked games are games of skill."

"And I take it they were out-classed?" Jessie asked.

"If you'll excuse the lack of humility, we weren't in the same league."

"And you won." Jessie wasn't really asking a question.

"Of course," Blain said proudly. "Again, forgiving my lack of humility, I took 'em for a ride. A real Sunday outing," he said, not hiding his satisfaction over the incident.

"And now they've come to return the favor," Jessie said, recalling her earlier speculation about Blain's involvement with the bandits.

"It appears that way."

"I see," she said as she thought it over.

"Why tell us about this now?" Ki asked.

The question confused the gambler. "I thought you should know."

"Any other reason?" Ki pressed.

Blain shrugged. "Well it seems unfortunate for us all to be in this predicament because of my affairs."

Jessie nodded. "Do you have a suggestion to make?"

"Much as I hate to suggest it—after all, I feel the money is mine—perhaps it would be better all around if I were to return some part of it."

"To the bandits?"

Blain nodded. "It just isn't going to do me any good if I die of thirst in the middle of this wasteland."

"You're willing to use the money to buy our freedom," Jessie said wanting to be sure they understood each other.

"I guess that's the long and short of it," Blain said, sticking his hands into his vest pockets.

"It doesn't bother you that Richards could be making the same offer with his money?" Jessie asked.

Blain smiled. "Well, sure I wouldn't mind, but seeing as how I got us into this fix . . ."

"What makes you so certain?" Ki asked.

"That they want their money back?" Blain looked confused.

"That it's you the bandits are after," Ki clarified.

"I never supposed otherwise."

"Why?"

"They swore they'd get even with me," Blain explained. "I never for a moment doubted them, and left early the next morning."

"And you recognized the bandits, or some of them, as the men you outfoxed?" Ki asked again.

"Well I couldn't actually see them," Blain said thoughtfully. "They were wearing masks and hats, but I naturally assumed . . . Two of them had the right build," he added.

"Which was . . . ?"

"A tall, scruffy fellow, and his shorter, squatter pardner."

Jessie let out a chuckle. "That description could fit almost any two range hands.''

"You don't think that maybe I was wrong, and that—"

"We don't know what to think," Ki said. "But we'll keep your offer in mind."

"Then what are you going to do?" Blain asked bluntly.

"First, I'm going to try and fetch us some water," Ki answered. "If you could bring me out the canteens that are inside, I'd appreciate it," Ki said.

"Right away," Blain said and left.

Jessie waited for him to get out of earshot before speaking. "You seem skeptical. Do you doubt his story?"

"Not at all," Ki answered, as he started saddling a horse. "But I wonder, if they were after him, why didn't they take back their money and beat the stuffing out of him when they first caught up to the wagon party?"

"So then we're back to square one." Jessie remarked, unable to argue with the inherent logic of Ki's question.

"Not necessarily. Oddly enough, we might have just eliminated one of our suspects."

"I thought we were no longer interested in suspects and secrets and who and why?"

"Did I say that?" Ki remarked with a grin.

Yvette came out carrying the canteens. "Blain said you were going for water."

"I am," Ki nodded.

"But I thought you didn't know where to go."

"I don't."

"Then how can you—"

"I don't know where the water is, but the bandits do. Either I'll take their water, or I'll get them to show me where the water is."

Yvette took Ki to be joking, and was about to say so, when she realized that he wasn't smiling. She turned to Jessie. "He's serious, isn't he?"

"It's the first I'm hearing of it," Jessie answered, "but he appears to be."

"But it's six against one," Yvette exclaimed.

"Two," Jessie corrected her.

Ki shook his head. "You stay here, Jessie."

"Take Evan with you," Yvette suggested. Though she agreed Ki shouldn't go alone, she thought Jessie shouldn't go with him.

Ki smiled, and addressed them both at once. "If I were to take anyone, I'd take Jessie. But it'll be safer to go alone. You know that," he said directly to Jessie.

"But it's still dangerous," Yvette protested.

"There's some risk," Ki admitted. "But not as much as you think. I suspect there'll only be one man awake, watching herd on us. The others should be asleep."

"Still, one man . . ." Yvette began.

"He'll be all right," Jessie assured her. "Ki can take care of himself."

"I seem to remember something of the sort," Yvette said as she recalled the way Ki surprised her the other night.

"See you in the morning," Ki said as he finished tying the canteens to the saddlehorn.

"There's another reason I came out here," Yvette began reluctantly.

Sensing the hesitation in her voice Jessie excused herself. "I'll leave you two alone." Yvette didn't argue, and Jessie left.

"Ki, I had to see you."

"Don't worry, nothing will happen," Ki said confidently.

"I'm starting to believe you," Yvette said with a smile. "But there's something I've been meaning to tell you."

"Wait here, and tell me when I get back."

Yvette thought it over and realized since she had waited this long there would be no harm in waiting a little longer. "I guess it'll hold." But she sounded uncertain.

She watched Ki swing up onto the horse. "You want me to wait for another reason don't you, Ki?"

Even in the dark, Ki could see her eyes twinkle seductively. "You've been on my mind since yesterday."

"I'll wait," she said breathlessly, "but hurry."

Chapter 10

Ki headed away from the depot, and away from where he thought the bandits were camped. He used the adobe building as cover till he was over the distant rise; then he swung in a large arc to his left. He continued in that direction till he was sure he had outflanked the bandits.

He then began to follow an imaginary grid, slowly walking his horse through one sector after the next. Ki hoped to come upon the group of sleeping brigands before he came upon their awake sentry. Of course the bandits could have been anywhere, but Ki assumed they positioned themselves to the front of the depot.

A few minutes later he was proven right when he saw his horse's ears prick up, and the animal's head turn to the left. The roan had picked up the smell of the bandits' horses.

Ki dismounted and tied his horse to a nearby tarbush, then slowly started in the direction his roan had indicated.

He heard the restlessness of the bandits' horses at about

the same time he saw them, ground-tied in a bunch of indian ricegrass. Though Ki's silent *ninja* approach would not disturb the sleeping men, there was nothing he could do to hide his smell from the animals. They stopped grazing once they picked up his scent, and now they fidgeted nervously.

Ki made his presence known to the animals, standing up straight and approaching slowly. He moved in a manner that would not startle them. As long as the horses didn't whinny there would be no problem. He continued to move towards them, all the while thinking calming thoughts. He made sure his whole being emanated a feeling of peace and gentility. His gaze focused first on one horse and then on the next, till he had made eye contact with all six of them. He could feel their nervousness fade, as their fidgeting stopped. They stood there watching him with their large, serene eyes.

Ki continued working his animal-charming techniques, a method taught in the Orient and known as *ninpo-inubue*. Presently the horses went back to grazing. Indifferent to Ki's presence, they lowered their heads and pulled at the clumps of densely tufted, leafy grass.

Ki now turned his attention to the men. Five yards past the bunchgrass he saw the sleeping forms of five men. Two were propped up against their saddles, the others had their saddles next to them. He couldn't help but notice the canteen that hung from one saddlehorn.

With a smile Ki moved forward and grabbed it. Then he went to around to each man, grabbing the canteen or waterbag that either hung from the saddle or lay next to it. He had just grabbed the last one when he heard a twig snap.

"Hey, you," a man's voice boomed out.

Ki had been so intent on moving quietly, and had been watching the sleeping men so closely, he had failed to hear the approach of the sixth bandit. Ki's hands were encumbered with the canteens, and the man was beyond the range of even a flying drop kick. The only alternative left to Ki was to make a run for it.

The bandit reached for his gun, and Ki swung his right arm. The last canteen, the one he had just picked up, went flying through the air. Ki didn't wait to see its effect, though from the solid thump and subsequent loud oath it must have hit its mark. There was also no gunshot, another testament that the canteen had done its job.

Ki dashed for freedom, but as he jumped over the last of the sleeping bodies, a hand reached up and grabbed his ankle. Facedown he fell to the dirt. Instinctively he knew better than to try and fight his way out. By now the bandits were surely awake and Ki didn't think it wise to go up against six gunmen. Instead he lay there a moment and gathered his wind.

"All right, fella, get up." A boot prodded his ribs none too gently.

Ki stood up slowly. Two men were already out of their bedrolls, guns drawn and at the ready. Two others were just crawling out. A tall, broad-shouldered man was approaching Ki.

The returning sentry, a stocky man with a flat face and a round forehead, was rubbing his head, and staring at Ki angrily. "I caught him red-handed."

"Good thing, too," one of his companions teased, "or he might have made off with all our gold."

"Shut up, Smith," the sentry replied. "You were sleeping sound as a baby while he was pryin' around."

"Well at least I weren't on the losing end of a fight with a canteen."

"I'm warning you, Smith," the sentry repeated, "shut your mouth."

"Aahh, you're all talk." the other taunted.

"Both of you shut up," the tall man ordered. He had

wide-set, dark eyes, a thin nose, and a long thick moustache. He was obviously the leader. He sized up Ki quickly. "You're not packin' a gun." It was not a question, and he continued without waiting for an answer. "Yet you come sneakin' in here in the middle of the night."

"What's the difference why he was pokin' his nose 'round here? I'm a gonna twist it plumb off his face," the angry sentry threatened.

"That's why I do the thinking, Carl," the leader informed him.

"You didn't get hit in the head...." Carl began defensively.

"Then try usin' yer head for somethin' other'n a target," the leader answered. "There are things to figure out before you go around fixin' someone's face."

"All right, boss, but when you're through with him..."

"We'll see." The boss turned his attention back to Ki. "All right, pardner, you do some talkin', or I let Carl have his fun with you."

Ki remained silent.

"Hell, shoot him an' let's get back to sleep," one of the bandits suggested.

"Well, pardner," the leader continued. "I ain't got all night. You'd best begin now."

Ki shrugged. "It's not a long story. I came to collect your canteens."

"You'd best come up with a better story than that," Carl snarled, "or you'll be sorry."

Ki ignored the threat.

"I think he's tellin' the truth," the boss said.

"You ain't gonna believe that, are you, Dan?" another bandit asked the leader.

Dan nodded. "It's obviously the truth. Carl caught him red-handed, an' there they are," he said, pointing to the pile of canteens that lay in the dirt.

"But why, and where'd he come from?" Carl wanted to know.

"You'd know if you were out there doin' yer job instead of sleepin'," Dan said accusingly.

"Boss, I wasn't sleepin'. I swear it."

Dan seemed unconcerned with the sentry's plea. "Look around," he said harshly. "There's only one place he could have come from, and only one reason why he'd be stealin' our water. Ain't that right, pardner?"

There was no reason to deny it, and Ki nodded.

"So now that you know, let me bust him in his face," Carl said eagerly.

"Not now," Dan answered. "And maybe not ever."

"But, boss . . ."

Another bandit agreed. "I don't see why Carl can't have some fun."

"Cause he's a valuable hostage," the boss answered.

"He'd be just as valuable with a broke nose," Carl continued to argue.

"Maybe you're right. But as long as I'm leading this outfit, you don't touch him." He looked challengingly at the others and waited for any arguments; there were none, and he continued. "Good. We want him in top shape. That way he'll fetch a top price," he said with a smile.

"What so special 'bout him, anyway?" Smith wanted to know.

"He's our ticket out of this waste-hole," the boss answered.

"I don't see what one skinny Chinee is gonna—" Carl began.

The leader smiled. "We have something that they want, and to get it back they give us something we want. No more waiting around."

Carl looked dubious. "What makes you think they give a plugged nickel 'bout what happens to him?"

109

The boss smiled menacingly. "They ain't like us," he explained simply. "None of them wants a man's death hangin' over their head. Now get some rope an' tie him up."

Carl crossed over to his saddle and picked up a length of rope. "I'll hog-tie him, but I ain't standin' watch over him; my shift's over."

"I can't watch him and the depot at the same time," Smith complained. Obviously he was to be the next sentry.

"I wouldn't worry too much about them folks holed up in that 'dobe," the boss began. "Until he gets back,"—he said with a nod towards Ki—"they ain't going nowhere."

"Then I'm just going to watch him," Smith said flatly. There were no objections.

Carl started to tie Ki. He reached for Ki's arms, momentarily stepping between his prisoner and the other bandits. There would not be a better opportunity, and Ki seized it. He extended his arms helpfully, but as soon as the bandit had his wrist, Ki quickly reversed the grip, grabbing the bandit instead. Ki threw his other arm around the surprised man's neck and pulled him in to him.

Ki moved so quickly that none of the other bandits realized what had happened until it was too late. When the situation did sink in, Ki already had Carl's gun plucked from the holster, and was pointing it at the bandits, while using the helpless sentry as a protective shield. Carl tried to struggle, but Ki's grip was tight, and the more the bandit wiggled the harder Ki's forearm dug into his Adam's apple. Out of necessity he stopped squirming and applied his efforts to simply breathing.

"Drop the guns," Ki ordered.

The bandits were slow in moving.

"Drop them and no one gets hurt," Ki repeated.

"You can't get us all," the boss said calmly.

Ki turned to him. "No, but I'll get you first."

"I ain't doubting you, friend," the boss said calmly, "but I reckon you won't be any better for it."

"You're all standing out in the open," Ki observed. "I have pretty good protection. You'll have to be a mighty sure shot to make sure you hit me and not—"

Smith's laugh cut him short. "We'll take that chance," he said cruelly.

Ki then realized he had made a serious mistake. There was enough animosity among the bandits that the risk of shooting one of their own was insignificant. Perhaps Smith was only bluffing, but Ki had no way of knowing.

"Question is, how good a shot are you?" one of the others asked. "You only got six bullets there. Think you can make each one count?"

"I think maybe you should drop your gun," the boss suggested with a smile. "Before you get hurt."

There seemed to be no other choice. Ki lowered the gun, and released his hold on Carl. For a moment the bandit rubbed his throat, but then he swung his fist viciously at Ki's face. Ki saw it coming but felt it was for the best to do nothing. He rolled with the punch, but even so the man's knuckle split his lip, and blood spurted forth.

Carl reared back to strike again but Dan crossed to him and grabbed his arm before he could deliver another blow. "That's enough," he ordered. "I don't want him hurt."

"You seem to care a hell of a lot more about this here stinkin' Chinaman than you do about me," Carl complained.

"Because right now he's of more use to me," Dan answered without hesitation.

Carl didn't seem pleased, but he picked up his gun and shoved it back into his holster. "I ain't forgettin'," he told Ki. "We got a score to settle," he added as he dropped down on his bedroll.

"All right. Let's finish what we started," the boss said. "Smith, tie him."

Ki didn't fail to notice that two bandits kept their guns trained right on him. This time he allowed himself to get tied.

The other men went back to their blankets and were soon asleep. Smith rolled a cigarette and smoked it leisurely, watching the smoke as it drifted in the moonlight. When he finished he tossed the butt aside, grabbed another rope and walked over to Ki. "I don't suppose you'll mind if I catch a few winks. But you make mention of it come mornin' an' I'll tan your hide good, no matter what Dan says 'bout it. Maybe I'll even let Carl have some fun, too."

"I won't say anything," Ki assured him. Ki could hope for nothing better than to have his guard go to sleep.

"Good. An' just in case you have any ideas . . ." Smith wrapped the rope around Ki, then uncoiled the rest of it and wrapped it around the horn of three saddles. "I don't think you'll drag those very far." Then he lay down and tied the end of the rope to his ankle. "But if I feel even the slightest tug . . ."

"You won't," Ki promised.

He was true to his word.

A master at *hoju-jutsu,* Oriental rope-binding techniques, Ki was also knowledgable in the various methods and means available to assist one in slipping free of those very same ropes. By flexing his wrist muscles, and by laying his hands together at an angle while they were being tied, he now had some slack to play with. He knew how to work the rope to stretch the fibers and loosen the knots. He was also able, thanks to the strength and dexterity in his fingers, to maneuver the rope down from his wrists to his hands. From there it was only a few more minutes till he had slipped his bonds.

Although he could have shimmied out of the rope that

was wrapped around his body, he found it more expedient to take a *shuriken* from his pocket and slice through it. He did the same with the rope around his ankles.

Throughout, he had made little noise, and the men remained fast asleep. For a moment Ki wondered if he could press his advantage. He could round up the bandits and perhaps solve this once and for all. But Ki realized that, as Blain would say, the odds were not in his favor. The bandits were too willing to take chances, and they seemed to have no misgivings about letting one of their own get shot, simply for the chance of plugging Ki. Ki wanted to get back to Jessie. He was beginning to think there was a better way of dealing with the situation. He decided it would be best to slip away quietly.

But Ki didn't want his mission to be a failure. He wasn't going to leave empty-handed. Silently he once again gathered up the canteens and waterskins. Most of them were where he had dropped them. One was where it had hit Carl; another had been picked up and replaced on a saddle.

This time, though, Ki had learned from his mistake. He moved just as slowly, just as quietly as before, but as he picked up the canteens he put them over his shoulder. He wanted to have one hand free at all times. It turned out to be a wise decision.

Ki had almost made it back to his horse when he heard a sound behind him. He immediately slipped his hand into his vest and grabbed a *shuriken*. His fingers barely closed on the sharp metal throwing star when he heard the voice behind him.

"Turn around, Chinaman. I ain't never shot a man in the back, and I don't plan on startin' now—not even on the likes of you."

Ki stopped short, and Carl let out a laugh. "You ain't the only hombre that can creep around Injun-style," the

113

bandit gloated. "I stayed awake waitin' for this chance. I knew you'd just be dumb enough to try somethin' stupid, an' I was right."

Carl was so pleased with himself that he seemed content to prattle on. Ki didn't mind, as it gave him the opportunity to slowly ease his hand out of his vest pocket.

The bandit continued, unaware of Ki's slight movements. "Yeh, I heard you sneakin' around, but it was all for nuthin', Chinaman. When I get through with you, you'll be lucky if'n you can crawl. Or maybe I'll just put a few slugs into your legs."

"Your boss won't like you taking matters into your own hands," Ki said. His hand was almost clear of his pocket.

"What could I do?" Carl said with a shrug. "It was either that or let you get away. In fact it'll be pretty good shootin' on my part that you ain't totally dead. What with you runnin' like a Comanche . . ."

"I'll tell him the truth," Ki argued. There was no point to his protest other than to buy another second or two.

"Friend, I owe you a debt," Carl said maliciously. "I just realized that for my story to hold water, I'm gonna have to plug you in the back of the legs. It'll look like you really was runnin'."

"Wait," Ki cried out in mock terror.

"A pity. I sure did want to see your face . . ."

Ki had a brief moment to decide. Should he play it defensively and dive to the side, putting most of his efforts into avoiding Carl's first shot, or should he be more aggressive and put his efforts into a precise throw of the *shuriken?* Ki knew it didn't have to be an either/or decision, but any evasive action on his part would only add to the inaccuracy of his throw. Ki had only one *shuriken;* Carl had six shots.

Ki heard the hammer of the gun cock, and he reacted. He twirled around and jumped high into the air. The simple leap with legs spread served his purpose best. It removed his principle target from the line of fire—he trusted that Carl was after all aiming for his legs—but it also allowed him to face his opponent, keeping sight of his target all the while.

His eyes focused in on Carl's wrist, and with a flick Ki sent the silver star whizzing on its way. The blade cut into flesh as the gun was being fired. It might have been a fraction of a second later, or perhaps a fraction early. It didn't matter; the shot missed, and the gun fell to the ground.

"You bastard!" Carl screamed in pain.

Ki didn't wait to hear the rest. It was a short dash to his horse; then he was gone.

Chapter 11

"I was so scared when I heard shots . . ." Yvette said excitedly the moment Ki rode into the shed.

"A little unexpected trouble," Ki began.

"But you're not hurt, are you?" Worry creeped into her voice.

Ki shook his head.

Yvette let out a sigh of relief. "What was it all about?" she wondered. But she didn't wait for an answer. She was overcome with emotion and could no longer control herself.

Though Ki started to explain, he found it difficult to talk with Yvette's lips pressed against his, and then he promptly lost his interest in doing so once he felt Yvette's breasts warm and soft against his chest. Any further possibility of discussion ended as blood flowed quickly into his now throbbing manhood.

"I'd really like to know what happened, Ki, but right now I think there are more urgent needs to take care of," she said as she ran her hand up his leg and brought it to rest on his growing bulge.

Before Ki realized it, his shaft was freed from the encumbering restraints of his jeans, and Yvette began lightly teasing him with her fingers. His member responded to her touch by growing even harder.

"It feels even better in my hand than it did brushing up against me when we were on the horse," she cooed in his ear. "And it felt pretty good then," she added with a smile.

"I feel obligated to agree," Ki said with a smile of his own, as he reached under her blouse to caress the soft skin of her breasts. His fingers glided over her nipples, and they in turn stiffened to his touch.

Yvette's breathing became harder, and Ki soon felt her warm breath move down his body to his crotch, where her moist lips encircled his shaft. He closed his eyes and gave himself to the sensation. Thoughts of bandits, bank tellers, and angry sentries faded into the distance, as did the recent problems that had crowded his mind. The cramped adobe room, stifling and dry, was no longer a reality. Yvette, running her warm, wet tongue over his manhood, was the only world he knew. His body reveled in the pleasure, drifting, relaxing for the first time in what seemed like an eternity.

Ki gave an involuntary shudder of delight, as Yvette's teeth grazed over his shaft. But his reverie lasted only a moment more. He suddenly realized that Jessie would be wondering where he was.

He opened his eyes. "Yvette," Ki began, "there's something I've got to do first."

"Is there something more important than feeling good?" she asked as her tongue flicked across his sensitive, tender skin.

Ki nodded. "I want to bring the canteens in to Jessie."

Yvette understood, and slowly she withdrew her mouth

from his organ. "She'll be worried too," she said. "She stood up and straightened her dress. "I'll be here."

Ki heard her soft moaning before he saw her stretched out on the warm dirt. She was lying facedown, and the round globes of her buttocks moved seductively in the air. Her hands seemed buried under her, but occasionally he saw flashes of her fingers as they slid between her legs.

For a moment he stood there transfixed, stunned by her feminine beauty and her sensuous movements. He watched her hips rock slowly back and forth as her legs stretched and flexed, the smooth lines of her thighs revealing the lean muscles that lay underneath her soft skin.

Ki could hear her breath—heavy, almost rasping—and her body started to rock with an increased urgency. Her movements started to pick up speed, and her hand, now clearly visible, kneaded her fleshly, moist mound.

Ki realized that he was also breathing quicker, and there was an almost painful throbbing in his loins. He quickly stepped out of his jeans.

"Ki? Is that you?" Yvette asked without stopping her steady grind against her hand.

"You look beautiful," was his answer.

"You've been watching me," she said with no anger in her accusation.

"Only for a moment," he answered as he moved closer and dropped to his knees.

"Don't make me wait, Ki. Please."

He brushed his erect shaft against the soft flesh of her backside. "You've already made me wait too long," she said with dry voice.

Yvette raised her hips a little higher into the air as a further inducement, but Ki needed no further encouragement. He slowly guided his pole to the entrance of her womanhood, where he paused briefly, feeling the soft hairs

119

tickle his pulsing member. He gently pressed forward, sliding easily into her opening.

Yvette let out a low moan. Ki swayed slightly backwards, rocking gently in and out of her.

"Ki, don't tease me," she said crossly. But Ki ignored her plea and continued his slow movements.

"It feels good, Ki, but I want to feel all of you."

"You will," Ki promised. "But right now I want you to relax and enjoy this."

"I am enjoying it," she protested. "But I'm way beyond relaxing. You don't understand . . ."

"Shh." Ki pulled back till the tip of his shaft was pressed against her.

Yvette let out a louder moan, and reached underneath her to grab his firm pole. She held it in place while she rocked her sensitive love-bud fervently against his hard flesh. It was as exciting to Ki as it was to her. When they could both stand it no longer Ki thrust his hips and sent his shaft deep inside of her.

She let out a gasp. "Maybe you do understand," she whispered contentedly. "Maybe you know exactly what I want."

Ki was pumping deep inside of her, and she met his every thrust. When Ki slid his hand under her and reached for her breast she moaned again. "You know me so well, Ki. You know how to make me feel so good."

Ki increased his rhythm, and Yvette was soon reduced to making gurgling sounds deep inside her throat. That she could no longer speak coherently excited Ki still further and he pistoned in and out of her with forceful strokes.

Her hips started to rock furiously, her back bucking against his body like a wild stallion. Only his strength and deep penetration kept them together. He could feel her body tense, and he grabbed at the pointed nipples of her swelling breasts.

120

Yvette's muffled gasp preceded her spasm by only a fraction of a second. Her legs jerked twice, and her body went rigid. Then she collapsed with a contented sigh.

"That's never happened to me before," Yvette said dreamily.

"I find that hard to believe," Ki said with a smile.

"No, it's true. I've been satisfied before," she added demurely, "but I'm usually the one in control." She reached behind her to stroke the inside of Ki's thigh. "And I never finish first."

Ki laughed. "I hope we're not finished."

"Roll over," Yvette ordered as she squirmed out from beneath him.

Ki did as he was told. Yvette leaned over and let her hair brush against his chest. Slowly she made her way down his torso till his hard manhood was entwined in her soft locks. She then lowered her head and engulfed his organ with her mouth. She sucked on it hungrily, letting her saliva flow down the shaft. She started bobbing her head up and down, taking his full length deep inside her throat.

Ki was soon moaning softly, moving his hips in time with her head. Yvette placed her hand around the base of Ki's organ and began to stroke it firmly while her tongue flicked lightly across the tip.

She raised her head but continued her hand motion. "Forgive me for stopping, Ki, and call me selfish if you'd like, but I have to feel you inside of me again."

"I don't think there's a man alive that would offer a complaint right now. . . ." His words trailed off into a soft sigh as Yvette straddled his pole and slowly lowered her body onto his.

"Now you just lie there, Ki, and let Yvette take you for a ride, a nice long ride."

Ki didn't resist. He did as he was told, enjoying not

only the pleasurable sensations, but admiring the woman's form and fluidity as well.

Yvette was clearly skilled in these matters. She placed her heels under her and in a squatting position, indeed behaving as if she were riding a stallion. A combination of raising and lowering her body while tilting her pelvis back and forth soon had Ki moaning in ecstasy.

Ki ran his fingers across Yvette's full breasts, sometimes barely touching the skin, at other times firmly massaging her heavy orbs. She reached up and pressed Ki's hands to her bosom as she let out a sigh.

"I shouldn't be liking this as much as you," she started to say.

"Why not?" Ki asked with a smile.

"Because this is for you," she explained.

Ki started to rotate his pelvis. Yvette let out a load moan. "It's for both of us," Ki corrected.

"I'm getting that sense," Yvette agreed, as she started to roll her hips faster and faster. She leaned forward and kissed Ki lightly on his neck. "You have incredible stamina," she whispered in his ear.

"If you're tired we can roll over," Ki suggested.

She nibbled on his earlobe. "I'm not tired, but I'm nearing that point where I'm going to lose control again. . . ."

"Let yourself go," Ki urged as he pumped his hips and drove his shaft into her.

Yvette smiled. "Soon I won't have a choice. But I sure would like you to come with me this time."

"Soon I won't have a choice either," Ki said with a smile of his own.

Knowing he was as excited as her only encouraged Yvette more. She sat up and leaned back, putting her whole weight down on Ki's rod. He tunneled deep inside of her, and she let out a gasp. "I haven't ever felt it like that," she said with a tremor in her voice.

Ki flexed his powerful hips, making sure he was penetrating her to the hilt.

"Oh, Ki . . ." was all she could say. But she reached behind her and took his manly pouch in her hands. She fondled it gently at first, but as her own excitement grew, her grip grew tighter, and her massaging hand more insistent.

"Don't make me wait any longer," she pleaded with him. Her request, though the same as before, now had a slightly different connotation. But Ki could not deny her now, any more than he could before. Especially with the way her body moved and her hand gripped. . . .

Suddenly her nails dug into Ki's flesh as her fingers tried to squeeze the pleasure out of him. It was not painful; in fact, it was quite the contrary. Ki let out a gasp and almost involuntarily contracted his hips. He felt his organ swell; then, at the point of bursting, he released.

Yvette gasped as her own body clamped around his wildly jerking shaft. The pressure of his release had sent her over the edge and her body was now wracked by its own intense wave of pleasure. It seemed as if it was never going to subside. When it did she melted down on to Ki's muscular chest. Her eyes closed, as she drifted away. . . .

"Ki, there's been something I've been trying to tell you," Yvette began. She was lying against his side, cradled in his strong arms. "I should have told you before; I even tried, but. . . ."

"There's nothing you have to tell me," he assured her. He had a feeling what she wanted to confess.

"Shush now an' listen."

"Your past is of no interest to me. Only the present matters," he said as he stroked her hair.

"You listen, then decide. I've what you could call a colorful past, Ki. What many might call off-color."

"I don't think any less of you."

She ignored him and continued. "I've been a dance-hall girl."

"If I said I thought so, would you be insulted?" Ki asked.

"Not exactly insulted . . ." she said with some confusion.

"You weren't the perfect portrait of a homesteader," Ki explained. "There was something in your demeanor and your dress."

Yvette nodded. "I guess I was dressed a mite fancy for a pioneer, frills and lace and such."

"And that twinkle in your eye said you weren't a stuffy society woman," he continued.

"Oh, Ki, now you're just trying to flatter a girl. I don't think I'd ever pass as a well-bred lady."

"You'd be surprised."

"Well, thank you," she said as she started to blush.

"I'm serious. Once you leave your dance-hall days behind . . ."

"Ki," she said hesitantly, "I don't just *dance* for money. . . ."

Ki laughed. "Do I seem that innocent?"

"Not at all. I just wanted you to realize what I meant by that."

"I do. And it doesn't bother me."

"Not even a little bit?"

Ki shook his head. "Why should it?"

"It would bother most other men. But then, I reckon you're not like most other men, are you?" she said as she ran her fingers across his strong chest. "And that wasn't a question," she added. "I can say for a fact you aren't like other men."

"And you're not like other dance-hall girls. And I can say that for a fact," Ki added with a smile.

"I'll bet you can," she kidded him. "Why, you never had to pay for a dance in your life."

He didn't argue. "You're different, Yvette," he repeated.

"I hope so," she said seriously.

"A new start, somewhere else . . ."

"That's what I'm hoping for, Ki. And that's what I want to talk to you about."

"Go ahead," he urged.

"As much as I want a new start, there are some who don't want me to leave."

"The owner of the dance hall?"

"Yes, but he's not the real problem. I guess it's one man in particular I'm talking about."

"Who?"

"It doesn't matter, but he would do anything to make sure I don't leave."

Ki was getting the idea. "Like hold up a wagon party?"

She nodded.

"The bandits were hired to keep you from getting away?"

"I wouldn't say they were hired," she began. "He's one of them. Dan Grey."

"Their leader," Ki remarked after recognizing the first name.

Yvette nodded again.

"I may be just a dance-hall girl, but he considers me his."

"I see."

"At first I was flattered. I saw his good looks and his powerful body, and all the other girls were jealous. Oh, I was such a fool."

"Then what happened?" Ki asked.

"For a while I thought I was living on Easy Street. But then one morning I woke up, and—what can I say, Ki? I just couldn't do it anymore. I wanted to get away, to start over again."

"And Dan Grey didn't want to let you leave."

"That's putting it mildly."

"I can understand," Ki said softly. "I wouldn't want you to leave either."

"But you wouldn't keep me against my will."

"No."

"And you wouldn't keep me a prisoner either, would you?"

"There'd be no point in it."

Yvette smiled. "You say it as if it were so obvious."

"Isn't it?"

"Not to Dan. I wasn't much better off than a prisoner in jail. Finally, I saw my chance and I took off."

"And you're certain Dan is trying to bring you back?"

"I am."

"Then why didn't he just take you?"

"You mean instead of harassing us like this?"

"It would be easier."

"I think it's his pride," Yvette said thoughtfully. "He wants me to come crawling back to him. And because he's afraid I won't, he's doing everything possible to make sure I have no other choices."

"And he doesn't care who he hurts along the way," Ki remarked.

"No, but I do, Ki. I don't want this to go on any longer. If I knew Stephen was going to get killed, I never would have tried to leave. It's not worth it."

She was on the verge of tears, and Ki pulled her closer to him. "You can't hold yourself guilty for the wrong that others do."

"But it's my fault. . . ."

"It's not. You have as much a right to go where you want and do what you want as anyone else."

"But . . ."

"Do you want to remain Dan Grey's concubine?"

"What do you mean?"

Ki smiled. "Concubine. It's a word from my native land. Do you want to be Dan's slave the rest of your life?"

"Of course not," she answered quickly.

"Then stop feeling guilty. You're doing what you have to do, and I'm going to help."

"You don't think I should give in, just to save the others?"

"No."

"But I wouldn't want anything to happen to them."

Ki laughed. "It's an admirable thought, Yvette."

"I'm serious, Ki."

"I know you are. That's why you're not like other dance-hall girls. In fact, that's why you're not like most other people."

"Still, that's little comfort to Evan, Blain and—"

Ki interrupted her. "I believe what you're saying, Yvette. But I think you should know that you're not the only one who feels responsible for our problems."

"Why do you say that?" she wondered.

Ki briefly told her about his conversation with the gambler. "And I might add that Richards probably thinks they're after his money, too. So I wouldn't feel solely responsible."

"But I am."

"Don't worry, we'll work it out," Ki promised her.

"Soon, I hope. I can't stand being in that hot room any longer."

"Then stay out here a little longer," he said as he cupped her breast in his hand.

"I'll stay here as long as you like, Ki."

Ki lowered his mouth to her pointed red nipple.

"Especially if you do that," she said with a sigh. "But, Ki, I am worried. . . ."

"Don't be. We'll settle this soon," he said as he rolled on top of her.

"How?"

"I don't know. But we'll figure it out when the time comes."

That time was rapidly approaching, and the solution was one that was going to shock them both.

★

Chapter 12

When morning came, Ki decided the next step was to have a group meeting. He waited till everyone was wide awake; then he announced, "It's high time we laid our cards on the table." He caught both Blain and Yvette looking at him curiously. "There's only one way we're going to pull out of this, and that's if we stand together."

"Speaking for myself, we're with you," Evan said excitedly. He was raring for action.

"That's all you can speak for," Buck said brusquely. "Till I hear what he has to say I ain't throwing my cards in."

Evan started to argue, but Ki cut him short. "Let him do as he pleases," Ki began. "That goes for all of you. If we stick together we have a better chance, but we don't want anyone to join in against his will." He looked at each of them in turn, then continued. "It's been obvious from the start that the bandits have wanted something from you that they just couldn't take."

His next words were cut off by the gunshots that came from outside.

"Looks like they might have just changed their minds," Blain noted.

They all hurried to the door and front windows. Fifty yards away the bandits were lined up in a row.

"It's time for a little palaver," Dan Gray shouted loudly.

"How do we know it's not a trick?" Evan asked the others in the depot. He got no answer, so he shouted out his question to the bandit leader.

"Send two men out, an' let the others keep you covered. We'll do the same and meet in the middle."

"That won't ensure their safety," Evan yelled back.

"It'd be suicide for us to try anything," the bandit leader answered. "With your guns trained on us, and us out in the open . . ."

"I think we should do it," Ki said to the others, though he was addressing Jessie specifically.

Blain and Richards both opposed the idea. Buck, after a moment of thought, said, "Why not." But Ki waited to hear what Jessie thought.

"I'm ready to take the chance," she said when the others had spoken.

"Good. That settles it."

"Not quite," Evan said. "We have to pick the two men."

"I'm going," Ki said firmly.

"No one would argue that," Evan continued. "I'll go too."

Jessie shook her head. "You stay here. I'll go."

"You can't be serious, Jessie."

"I am."

"But, despite their assurances, you could get hurt."

"Still, I'm going," Jessie said firmly.

Even looked at Ki for support, but he got none. "Don't you realize how dangerous it is to go out there?"

"That's why I want to go. I want to be there if Ki needs me."

"You're not joking," Evan said, dumbfounded. He turned again to Ki. "You can't let her—"

"Your mind's made up, Jessie?" Ki asked.

Jessie nodded.

"Then even if I agreed with you, Evan, I'm afraid that's it," Ki remarked. "But she can handle herself," he informed the shocked man, "and from a strategic point of view it makes sense."

"I don't see what sense it makes sending a woman out to face bandits," Evan grumbled.

Ki explained. "The bandits know how many there are in our party, or they can guess pretty accurately. And they know there's at least one woman among us."

"I'll grant you that," Evan said. "But I don't see how that justifies letting Jessie go."

"Because if Jessie comes with me, they know there's another man back here behind a gun."

"I see," Evan mumbled.

"And that alone might discourage them from trying anything."

"But you say Jessie's as good a shot as any man," Evan said quickly.

"She is."

"Then she could stay here and man a gun."

"She could," Ki replied, "but the bandits don't know that she's an excellent shot. They'd just know that since there are two men out there, there's got to be one less back in here."

Evan admitted defeat. "I don't like it any more, but I can see it's no use."

"Don't worry," Jessie said sweetly. "Just keep your powder dry and your sights clean," she added with a smile. Then she turned to Ki. "Let's go."

They met Dan Grey and one of the unnamed bandits out in the middle of the basin. Ki had insisted they ride in on horseback. First, it would put them on an equal footing with the bandits, who were astride their own horses; and secondly, and perhaps more importantly, if trouble did arise they would have the animals as both a means of escape and partial cover.

"Well, friend, glad to see you made it unhurt," the leader said first. "Carl was sure he had winged you." Ki could detect no sarcasm in his voice, and he simply nodded. The bandit then turned his attention to Jessie, and smiled charmingly. "Ma'am, I offer my apologies for puttin' you all out like this, but you see there's something of mine you have that I'd like back."

Jessie was not taken in by the man's congeniality. Ki had informed her of the situation, and she had a word or two to say to the man. "The days are long gone when a woman can be considered a man's property."

Dan laughed. "Some other time and place I might argue that, ma'am, but right now I'd just as soon take what I feel's mine."

"We won't let you." Jessie remained firm.

"Ma'am, maybe you don't understand," he continued. "It don't look like you all have a choice."

"If that's true, then why have this little talk?" she countered.

"Because it ain't like me to let innocent people suffer."

"Your good intentions aside, Mr. Grey, I think there's more to it than that."

Again the bandit laughed. "If'n my heart wasn't spoken for, I do believe I'd feel something special for you, ma'am."

"And I feel nothing but contempt for someone who keeps a person against her will," Jessie shot back.

Dan turned to his partner. "She's a fiesty one, she is. But she doesn't realize what's at stake."

"I think she does," Ki said flatly.

Grey's eyes turned mean. "You'll die in that 'dobe if I don't get what I want."

"And if we do, you'll never get what you want," Jessie said coolly.

"You'll die a miserable death, clawing at your throats for lack of water. . . ."

"And you might find it hard gathering water yourself," Ki said with a smirk.

The bandit glared at Ki. Just when he seemed about to burst into anger, a smile crossed his face. "I reckon we've got ourselves smack in the middle of a Mexican standoff."

"Which is what we came out here to discuss," Jessie said flatly.

"Fair enough," agreed Grey. "But I feel it's only fair to say that, like our friend here, who made sure he'd get our canteens, I also get what I want. And I happen to have an ace up my sleeve."

Suddenly a shot rang out. Ki thought it came from behind him, from inside the adobe building, but he wasn't taking any chances. He moved his horse between Jessie and the two bandits.

There were more shots, in quick succession, coming from both sides. Ki was instantly wary about being caught in a deadly cross-fire. The bandits also assessed the situation similarly, but they seemed less inclined to flee. Perhaps they didn't feel threatened by Ki, who wore no gun, and Jessie, who was a woman; for they chose to join the fight and participate from where they were instead of retreating to their own lines.

When Ki saw Grey reach for his gun their option of running for safety was out of the question. He and Jessie could not have made five yards before they would be cut down by the bandit's bullets.

Before Grey's gun could clear his holster, Ki dove off his horse and slammed into the man. Though he didn't hit with much impact there was sufficient force to unseat the bandit, and they both tumbled to the ground.

At the first shot, Jessie's attention had immediately turned to the second bandit. He had seemed surprised by the gunshot, but he would no doubt recover in a moment, and Jessie was certain he, too, would be reaching for his gun. Her hand dropped quickly to her holster. But before she could level her gun, Ki stepped between her and her target. Though it blocked her from the bandit's gun, it also ruined her line of fire.

When that line of sight cleared a moment later, Jessie realized she was at a serious disadvantage. She had not gotten a bead on the bandit, particularly because she was hesitant to shoot first and ask questions later. She didn't want to shoot the bandit till she saw that his intention was to fire first on her. She knew, though, that he would not be subject to any such considerations.

And as Ki hurled himself onto Grey, Jessie saw that the bandit did have his gun drawn and pointed at her. She too had only once choice; she slipped her feet from the stirrups, and threw herself to the ground.

She heard the gun explode the second she hit the dirt. For the moment, she knew, she was safe; her horse was now blocking the bandit's line of fire. She quickly rolled to her knees and steadied herself.

The bandit fired again, blindly. His second shot caused her horse to bolt, and she now had a clean view of the bandit. But he also had a clear line of sight. He lowered the barrel of his gun, but he never got the chance to fire it.

Jessie squeezed off two quick shots. The second one went wild, hitting nothing, mainly because there was no target to hit. Her first shot had unhorsed the man, and he lay face down in a pool of his own blood. Jessie didn't know if he were dead or alive; it didn't matter. He wasn't moving; he wouldn't fire his gun again.

She turned to Ki. He was struggling with the leader, and the two rolled over each other. She wanted to help, but the two men exchanged places so quickly and frequently that she dared not intercede. But she couldn't leave until she knew Ki was safe.

Dan Grey was an experienced brawler. Even so, Ki would have had no difficulty with him if they had started out on an equal footing. But the moment they hit the ground, Ki's main advantage was nullified. In this rolling, rough-and-tumble brawl, Ki couldn't make proper use of his martial-arts skills. One of his most potent weapons, his feet, were useless, and his hands, equally as dangerous, were pinned to his side by his strong opponent.

This was not to say that Ki was helpless. He was skilled in wrestling and close-in fighting, but so was Grey. And the man was strong. Perhaps as strong as Ki. And he, too, knew the rules of this type of wrestling match.

Ki's main approach to this kind of fighting was to use his opponent's strength against him. Rather than match each move force for force, or try to resist every effort of his opponent, he would go with the movements, waiting for a subtle shift in balance to gain the upper hand. Unfortunately, Grey had the same philosophy. Every time Ki felt he gained an advantage, Grey turned it around.

They also both knew enough about dirty, back-alley fighting to cancel each other out. So the fight continued this way, with Ki on top one moment and Grey winding up on top the next. Both men appeared to have enough strength to keep this up endlessly. And that was when Ki hit upon a solution. He held an advantage that he just now realized.

135

Grey was unaware of Ki's skill in the martial arts; Ki had never used any in the man's presence. The fighting now was simple brawling, which required skill, but certainly did not exhibit any of the finesse or deadly ability that Ki had at his disposal.

Ki began to feign tiredness. He put up less of a struggle. He let Grey have a slight advantage. He did it gradually, so as to appear believable. Then, after a few more tussles, Ki relaxed for a moment. Grey seized his chance as Ki expected he would. The bandit lashed out with a strong right to the face. Ki saw it coming, and rolled with the punch. Even so, it stung, and left his ears ringing.

Grey could sense victory. He clambered to his feet, dragging Ki up with him. Again, Ki expected it. It was much easier to deal a knockout punch when one was standing, able to get the full force of the body behind the blow, than when one was lying down. Grey knew that, and was no doubt planning to end this quickly. Ki had put up a good fight but was obviously tuckered out and ready to be put away.

And that's exactly what Ki wanted his opponent to think. Grey was just reaching back, ready to strike, when Ki snapped out his leg in a lightning-quick *mae-geri-keage*. The kick struck Grey hard in the solar plexus, and momentarily startled him.

Now that they were standing, they were both prey to the gunfire that was whizzing by them from both sides. Ki was as anxious to end this fight as Grey was, and now he saw his opportunity. While the bandit was still surprised Ki leapt into the air. Ki put all his efforts behind one powerful *mae-tobi-geri*.

His foot exploded in Grey's face, and the bandit stumbled backwards. The next moment he spun around and fell to the ground. Powerful as his flying kick was, Ki knew it wouldn't have had that effect on him. Neither would it have caused Grey's shirt to turn a bright red below the shoulder, as it was now doing. Grey had been struck by a bullet.

Inside the depot, Evan heard the gunshot boom loud in his ears. He turned to Buck. "What are you shooting at?" he asked quickly.

"Didn't you see it? They went for their guns," Buck snapped back.

In truth Evan saw nothing of the kind, but now it was too late. The bandits were returning their fire, and all hell had broken loose.

One bandit was already down, and the others were scattering. But Even was keeping his eyes on Jessie. He had his gun ready, but there was no way to get a shot in; the risk of hitting her or Ki was too great. He had to look on helplessly while he watched her go down. But his heart started pumping again when he saw she was not hurt. Then, with sudden understanding, he realized that Ki was right when he said she could take care of herself. She certainly made fast work of the bandit as she blew him off his horse.

Blain and Richards were pumping enough shells into the bandits to keep them busy, so Evan turned his attention now to Ki. Again he had no choice but to watch helplessly. But it was a good thing he did. When he heard Buck's gun go off, then saw the bandit leader fall, he put two and two together.

He turned angrily to Buck. "Are you crazy?" he shouted. "You might have hit Ki."

"Mind yer business," Buck yelled back.

"I don't think you cared who you hit," Evan accused, as he moved to pull him away from the window.

Buck wheeled on him, and brought the butt of his revolver crashing into Evan's jaw. The homesteader never saw it coming, and he went down like a sack of potatoes.

Buck turned to Blain. "Drop it," he ordered.

The gambler was so intent on firing he didn't hear Buck. Buck grabbed Blain's shoulder and spun him around. "Drop it," he repeated.

Blain looked confused, but there was no arguing with the Colt .44 that was staring him in the gut. He dropped his gun.

Richards saw what was going on, and had a moment of indecision. Buck noticed and smiled. "Go ahead," he prodded. "I'd like nothing more." Without another word, Richards, too, dropped his gun.

Without taking his eyes off of the two men, Buck addressed Yvette. "Get over by the door, and don't try anything. Or someone will get shot."

Ki crawled over to Jessie. "Are you all right?" he started to ask, but stopped. He could see that she was. "I think the safest thing for us is to just stay put till one side retreats and the shooting stops."

Jessie nodded. "I saw what happens if you stand up for too long." She was referring to Grey.

"That bullet could have been meant for either one of us."

"You don't know which side it came from?"

"Unfortunately, I do," Ki answered. "He was shot from the back. It came from the depot."

"Then why do you think it could have been meant for you?"

"He staggered back when my kick struck. A moment earlier it might have been a clear shot at me."

"But why?" Jessie asked. "Then she answered it herself. "Buck?"

"It seems likely."

"But—"

138

A shout from the depot ended the conversation. It was Buck's voice.

"Hold your fire. It's all over, Dan. We're coming out."

The door opened and out stepped Blain, Evan, Richards and Yvette. They all had their hands over their heads. Buck was behind them, a revolver in each hand.

Chapter 13

"I don't like the looks of this," Ki said aloud.

Jessie agreed as she trained her gun on Buck.

Whether he saw her do this or had just guessed that she would, Buck directed his next comments to her. "I wouldn't even think about it, Jessie, lest you want these people to get hurt. Now both of you stand up easy, and make sure you leave the gun in the dirt."

Jessie and Ki did as they were told.

"All right, boys, up," he shouted to the bandits.

Dan had predicted it would have been suicide for the bandits, out in the open and unprotected as they were, to start trouble. And that was exactly the way it turned out. Only one man stood up—Carl.

But a moment later Dan pulled himself up, holding his injured left shoulder. "Damn it, Buck," he said angrily. "What took you so long?"

Buck shrugged.

"And why in hell didn't you do something before they

141

nearly killed us all?" the bandit leader demanded.

" 'Taint my concern," Buck said indifferently.

"Damn you," Dan said, and started to move towards him.

Buck shifted one gun to cover the bandit leader. "Hold it there, Dan. I'd hate to put another slug into you."

"You!" Dan's one word was filled with rage and hatred.

"I would have been happier to have hit him," Buck said with a nod towards Ki. "But . . ." he ended with a shrug.

"Don't, Carl," Buck snarled. The bandit was slowly reaching for his gun. "I don't care one way or the other, but I imagine for yer sake you'd prefer to toss it away than die with it in yer hands."

There wasn't much to think about. With a nasty oath Carl threw his gun aside.

"So much for your ace in the hole," Jessie remarked. She turned to Buck. "So you're part of the outlaw band."

To her surprise, Buck denied it. "I ain't part of nothin'. I'm my own man."

"Then what are you trying to pull?" Evan asked.

"I think one might call it a double-cross," he said simply.

"There's still time to reconsider," Dan broke in. "Little harm's been done. Put down that gun, I'll take what I came for, an' me an' Carl'll hit the wind."

"I don't know, pardner . . ." Buck began.

"You fool. I'll get you for this," Dan snapped.

"That's what I'm afraid of. I don't think you take lightly to being crossed. I don't think you'll let me ride out of here, especially when you find out what I'm ridin' out with."

"I'll kill you . . ." Dan began.

"Easy, there. I ain't talkin' 'bout yer woman. There's money here. More money than yer little whore is worth."

At the word *whore,* Dan's anger rose noticeably; his

face flushed and his jaw tightened. He could barely control himself. Only the Colt pointed straight at him kept him from lunging at Buck.

Richards was also stung by Buck's words. At the mention of his money he turned white.

Buck saw the bank teller's unease and smiled. "See, Dan, while all you wanted me to do was keep an eye on her, I discovered there was a pack of money travelin' with her. Money that I decided was going to be mine."

"It's mine," Richards shouted. "You can't."

Buck laughed. "I already did. Last night when you were sleeping."

"No, you're lying," Richards said frantically.

Ki saw right through the ploy, and tried to stop the teller. "Don't, Richards, it's a trap."

But his words were too late. The bank teller made a beeline for the battered, weather-beaten water trough.

Buck let out another laugh, and only then did Richards realize he had been tricked. Still, as if to reassure himself, or perhaps touch his cherished property one last time, he dug out the leather pack.

"I thank you," Buck smirked. "It would have been much more difficult without your help." Cautiously, keeping an eye on the rest of the group, he walked over to the teller. "Now hand it over."

Richards was shaking his head, clutching the pack tight to his chest.

"Don't be a fool," Jessie advised. "Give it to him."

"I won't."

"I ain't even gonna bother askin'," Buck threatened. "You can hand it to me now, or I can take it three seconds from now." He thumbed back the hammer on one of his two revolvers. "A dead person doesn't have a very strong grip."

"All right. It's yours," the teller conceded.

143

Whether it was premeditated or simply done out of anger and frustration would never be known, but Richards flung the pack at Buck's head. The gunman was momentarily taken by surprise. Richards saw this, and suddenly dove at the man.

The bag hit Buck in the face, and he stumbled back a half step. Then the pack fell away, and Buck could clearly see the teller flying through the air, coming directly at him.

The gun in his hand exploded twice.

The force of the bullets on impact stopped Richards's forward movement. The teller fell face down into the dirt —or rather, he fell on what was once his face. At that range the .44 cartridges had blown away most of the man's features.

Yvette let out a sharp scream and covered her eyes.

"You didn't have to kill him," Blain said sharply. "He was harmless."

"It was a fittin' end for the little skunk," Buck snarled. Then he coolly picked up the pack and turned back to the others. "Anyone else like to try anything? I thought not."

"Is that what you have planned for the rest of us?" Evan asked.

"It can be arranged," was Buck's answer.

"If we were to rush you all at once, you'd be helpless." Evan continued.

"You're welcome to try," Buck did not seem too worried.

"I think we're going to wind up the same way, regardless of what we try," Evan answered.

"Like I said, it don't matter much to me. I got enough bullets left to take care of any of you stupid enough . . ."

"How do you know? You may not have as many as you thought. It'd be pretty hard to keep track with all this shootin' going on."

"That's the difference between us, pardner. You live by

the shovel in yer hands, and I live by these." He waved the two Colt revolvers. "I know how many times these guns have gone off."

"Can you be sure?"

"I don't have to be." Buck said calmly. "I ain't lookin' down their barrels. But just so you don't go try somethin' stupid too, I'll tell you there are nine shells left. One hit Dan, and two went into our friend over there."

Ki didn't think Evan's statements would have any effect on the situation, but he was glad the exchange was taking place. It gave him time to slowly, unnoticeably, slip his hand into his vest pocket. But he came up empty-handed.

His ever-present *shuriken* were absent. True, he had already used one, but there should have been many others in there. They must have fallen out in his fight with Grey.

Ki began to feel uneasy.

And the feeling grew worse when Buck issued his next orders. "Everyone face up against the wall—except you two women."

Ki started back to the building, and Evan fell in beside him. "We could try rushing him," he whispered.

Ki shook his head almost imperceptibly. "It's too risky. Jessie or Yvette could get hurt."

"But we have to do something."

"As long as they could be endangered by our actions we do nothing."

"But they're in danger now," Evan said with urgency.

Ki was well aware of that. He had nothing more to say.

"Ki . . ."

"We wait."

"Get yer noses into that wall and yer hands up high," Buck continued. "You stay here, Jessie, where I can keep an eye on you. And you," he said to Yvette, "bring round the horses."

When Yvette returned with the animals he instructed

Jessie to hold the horses, then told Yvette to fetch the saddles.

"I can't manage them alone," the woman complained. "They're too heavy."

"You best figure out a way. Drag 'em if you have to. But if you ain't back here in a minute I'm gonna start taking target practice at that wall."

Yvette hurried off and came back dragging a saddle.

"Now the other one," Buck ordered. There was no mistaking the implication.

This time Blain spoke out. "You have the money, Buck, why not just take the horses and high-tail it out of here?"

"Keep yer nose to that wall or I'll shoot it off," Buck snapped.

Blain quickly turned around. "You hold all the cards, Buck; don't play it dumb."

Buck laughed. "I do indeed hold all the cards. Dan thought I was his ace in the hole, but I turned out to be the joker in the deck. An' joker's wild in this game."

Blain tried one more time. "We don't give a damn 'bout Richards or his money. You won the pot, but—"

"I'm the big winner," Buck said with a laugh. "An' that's why I'm takin' the queen of hearts with me. Ain't that what gamblin's all about? You win big or you lose big . . ."

"The game ain't over yet," Dan said defiantly.

"Unless you got another card to play, I say it is," Buck said calmly.

Yvette returned with the second saddle and Buck instructed Jessie to saddle the horses. "An' just in case you forgot," he warned her, "anythin', anythin' at all I don't like, and I start shootin'." He chuckled nastily, then added, "And boyfriend there gets it first."

Jessie didn't know if he was referring to Evan or Ki. But either way it didn't matter. She did not plan to provoke

Buck into firing on any of them. Though her mind had been racing, looking for an opening, a way out, it now stopped abruptly.

She threw the saddle across the horse, briefly considering doing a sloppy job. She recalled what had happened to Richards when he tried to escape that first night on a saddle whose girth wasn't sufficiently tightened. But Buck was an experienced rider; it wouldn't work. She also didn't like to think how Buck would react if he found out she had attempted to trick him.

Until she could think of something foolproof, she was going to do as she was told. When she finished, Buck told her to stand to the side, then ordered Yvette to mount up.

"Don't do it," Dan shouted in anger. It wasn't clear whether he was addressing Yvette or Buck.

"Shut up," Buck snapped.

Yvette stood immobile, not knowing what to do.

This time Dan clearly spoke to her. "Don't worry, he won't harm you," he said as he turned around.

Yvette remained frozen.

Buck's next words shocked her out of it. "He's right. I won't hurt you, if you do as I say. If'n you don't, I start shootin'—at them."

Yvette grabbed the saddle and put her foot in the stirrup.

"You touch her and I'll kill you," Dan started to rave. "I swear it. I'll find you wherever you are."

"You're more'n welcome to try," was Buck's response.

"I'll rip your innards out with my bare hands."

Buck chuckled. "I sincerely believe you'll try," he said as he swung up into the saddle.

"You won't get away . . . ."

"We'll see about that."

"As long as I live I'll hunt you."

Buck stared him stared him straight in the eye. "I'm beginning to believe you, pardner."

"You'd best believe it," Dan fired back.

"Trouble is, you're in no position to be hurling threats," Buck said calmly.

"Ain't a threat," the bandit leader said with solid conviction. "You ride out of here with her, an' you're a dead man."

Buck swiveled slightly in the saddle and laughed haughtily.

"I swear it." Dan said firmly. "As long as I breathe, you'll—"

The crack of the Colt cut off his words.

Buck had slowly raised his gun and fired it, and Dan Grey slumped down against the wall, a large red stain spreading across his chest.

"See, pardner, I believed you after all," Buck said coolly. "So much so that I saw no reason to make life hard on myself. In the end this saved us both a lot of trouble," he added casually.

Buck turned to Yvette. "Now there's no reason to take you after all. Get down."

Yvette slid off the horse and raced to Dan. She dropped to her knees and took his head in her lap. "You fool," she said with tears in her eyes.

He was still breathing, though barely. A faint smile crossed his lips. "I knew you'd come back," he said weakly.

"Hush, don't try an' speak," she said as she brushed his hair from his forehead.

"That's all I wanted, for you to come back on your own."

"I'm here, Dan. And I won't leave you, ever."

148

His smile grew. "Was it wrong, Eve, to want you that much?"

"No." Her voice was thick and raspy.

"Good," he whispered as he closed his eyes.

She bent over and pressed her lips against his, but Dan Grey had already taken his last breath.

Things did not get any better. Buck suddenly turned to Jessie. "All right, your turn. Get up on that horse. Now." He turned to Ki. "Any objections?" he asked with a cold laugh.

Though Ki was facing the wall he knew Buck was looking straight at him. He also knew better than to protest. But that was the difference between Ki and men like Grey. Ki could channel his anger. He didn't have to curse, yell or make threats.

He had made a simple promise to himself years ago. A promise concerning Jessie and her safety. A promise directed at those who wished to harm her. Dan Grey was absolutely correct about one thing. If and when Buck rode out with Jessie, he could be signing his own death warrant. And Ki was judge, jury, and executioner.

"I don't reckon I heard you, Ki," Buck taunted. "Ain't you got nothin' to say?"

Ki remained silent. Next time they met he would let his actions speak for him.

Buck continued with business. "One last thing, Yvette, if you could be so kind as to tear yourself away. . ."

"You're an animal," she hissed.

"Get over here."

"Do as he says," Ki whispered.

She nodded and went over to him. He threw her a short rope and told her to tie Jessie's hand to the saddlehorn. "And they better be tight," he warned.

When it was done, Buck offered one last warning.

"There ain't much you can do to stop me, an' you won't be able to follow me on foot, so I ain't too concerned, but just in case any of you harbor sentiments akin to ol' Dan's there, and you vow to settle the score, just remember, she'll get it first."

He grabbed the reins of Jessie's horse, and with a brief *"Adios,"* spurred his horse forward.

On the far ridge, an interested spectator lowered his field glasses. All morning he had been keenly watching the shenanigans that were taking place down at the abandoned Overland depot. Now with a grim satisfaction, he decided the time for watching had come to an end. He spat a long stream of dark tobacco juice. Then his lips exposed an irregular row of cracked, stained teeth, as they spread into a smile of sorts. It was now time to act.

Chapter 14

There was no time to waste. Amidst fear and confusion, Ki immediately took command.

"See to Richards and Grey," he told Evan. "I'm starting out after Buck."

"You can't go after them on foot," Evan began.

"Maybe I won't have to," Ki answered. "The bandits' horses might be grazing right over that ridge."

"I'll come with you."

Ki shook his head. "Get those men buried. Then, after I round up the horses, we'll be ready to leave."

He started off at a jog, but Carl blocked his way. "Not so fast, Chinaman."

"Move," Ki ordered.

"Make me," Carl answered as he pulled a hunting knife out of his boot top.

"Why didn't you use that earlier, on Buck?" Ki asked. "You could have saved lives."

"Maybe I didn't get a chance, and then again maybe I just didn't care to."

"But he killed two men."

"It's no concern of mine," Carl answered. "But you are. I swore I wouldn't forget, and now that Dan's out of the way, we got a score to settle."

"Put down the knife and get out of my way," Ki repeated.

Carl laughed. "You're in no position to tell me what to do. Not while I got this." He slashed the knife at Ki.

Ki jumped back. Carl came at him again. And Ki stepped to the side. From the way Carl wielded the knife, Ki could tell he was experienced with the weapon. Ki backed up some more and studied his opponent.

Carl's obvious weakness was his bandaged wrist. The wound, inflicted just yesterday by Ki's *shuriken*, would hardly have healed by today. It no doubt took great effort for Carl to keep a firm grip on the knife. A few well-aimed blows should quickly bring the fight to a close.

Ki circled, waiting for his chance. As easy as it appeared, Ki did not want to rush things. If his judgment erred just slightly the consequences would be severe. A second off in his timing, or an inch off in his placement, and the blade would cut him. There was also the possibility that even if Ki's strike was perfect the knife, by a freak chance, would cut him as it flew from Carl's hand. Ki continued to watch his opponent carefully.

There was also the first rule of fighting to remember. When going up against an adversary who was better armed than oneself, one must always allow for "luck." A lucky punch or kick was one thing; a lucky shot or stab was something else entirely.

"Not so brave now that I have this," Carl said as he lunged again.

Ki stepped to the side and brought his hand down in a

chopping motion. The *tegatana-uchi* missed the wrist, hitting higher up on the forearm. Still, it struck with force and Carl let out a loud howl.

Carl snarled. "It's going to be a real treat to carve you up like a Sunday roast," he said as he feinted a lunge.

For a moment Ki began to reconsider his strategy. Carl was all offense. It had never dawned on him that Ki would mount any kind of attack. His stance was wide open, and left him vulnerable to blows to the body.

Without further thought Ki whipped out his leg and snapped it high into Carl's chest. Ki brought his leg back quickly before Carl could attempt to slash it with his blade.

The move was a mistake. It did little damage. Carl was a solidly-built individual, and it only served to make the bandit more cautious.

Ki's error only made him more impatient—a trait uncommon to him, especially while fighting. He repressed his desire to rush Carl with a fury of snap-kicks. Though he thought the onslaught would be successful, there was a good chance his leg would get cut in the process.

Ordinarily that would not bother him. With his legs rapidly moving in and out the wound would only be minor. But even a minor cut would be a serious disadvantage when it came to recovering Jessie. And that was his ultimate goal. Carl and the knife was only a temporary obstacle. He wanted to be in top shape to track and then face Buck. Therefore, he acted a bit more cautiously than he normally would have.

Carl mistook Ki's care as a sign of fear, and started to once again act more boldly. In fact he laughed off Ki's kick. "A lucky kick there, Chinaman, but you won't be lucky twice."

Ki was thinking the same thing about the bandit. He was eagerly awaiting the man's next lunge so he could counter with another chop to Carl's wounded wrist. This time he would not miss.

"In fact, Chinaman, the only luck you'll ever see is if I decide to go easy on you and kill you quickly." Carl continued a running patter of verbal abuse. It was supposed to rattle and unnerve his opponent, but it was having no such effect.

Ki grew even more focused on the wrist that held the knife. He was tired of this waste of time.

"Drop it," Evan suddenly said. He had seen the two men fighting and rushed over.

Carl ignored the command.

"Drop it or I'll shoot," Evan repeated. But his voice seemed to lack conviction. He was not the type who could easily shoot a man.

"I can take care of him," Ki said without moving his eyes from Carl's wrist.

Blain now also rushed up. "Better drop it. Even if you do manage to stick Ki, we'll never let you get away."

"Chinaman says he can take care of himself; let him." Carl answered.

"Drop it before there's any harm done," Blain continued.

"You going to shoot, you best do it now," Carl said with contempt. He had judged the two men fairly accurately; they weren't cold killers.

Blain tried one last time. "There ain't no future in this for you, friend. . . ."

"There's no future for him," Carl snapped.

"Don't do it," Evan said nervously.

Something in the tone of Evan's voice told Carl he was pressing his luck too far. If he was going to act it had to be soon. "You're one dead Chinaman," he growled then rushed Ki.

Evan's gun exploded, and Carl pitched forward. Ki, still

154

wary of the knife, grabbed the bandit's wrist and wrenched the blade out of Carl's grasp. It wasn't difficult. As Buck had said earlier to Richards, dead men don't have much strength.

"Are you okay?" Blain asked automatically.

Ki nodded. "He was no threat."

"I'm sorry," Evan began, obviously shook up. "I didn't know..."

"Don't feel any remorse," Ki said.

Blain agreed. "I wouldn't waste any tears on that sort."

"I'm not. In fact, I should have done that right from the start," Evan said strongly.

Both Ki and Blain were surprised by his change of attitude.

Evan explained. "I do believe you could have handled him," he said to Ki, "but why take the chance? Every minute we delay, Jessie and Buck get further away."

"You're absolutely right," Ki said. "Let's look for those horses."

"By the way, where did you get the guns?" Ki asked as they walked across to the ridge.

"When Buck drew on us, he had us drop our guns. These two were still sitting there right on the floor," Evan answered.

They weren't as lucky with the horses. The bandits' animals were nowhere to be seen.

"Well, that settles that," Evan said disheartedly.

"I'll have to start out on foot," Ki said.

"What's the use of that? You won't get very far."

"You'd be surprised," Ki answered.

"I don't much see the point in it, but I reckon there's not much more we can do." Evan wasn't sounding optimistic.

"Buck won't be expecting any pursuit; that gives us an advantage," Ki explained.

"Buck has a horse; that more than cancels our advantage," Even said sourly.

"One can cover a lot of ground on foot."

"I'm ready," Evan said.

Ki shook his head. "I'll make better time alone," he began.

"I'll keep up," Evan protested.

"No. I want you to stay here in case the horses return. There's a good chance Buck didn't take them with him. He might have just run them a few miles."

"It's not something I'd want to bet on," Evan answered.

"Even if he took them with him, there's still Grey's horse. During our tussle, it took off. Maybe Buck missed it and it will come back."

"I reckon we got no other choice. If and when these horses do show their hides, how will I find you?" Evan asked.

"Simple," Ki answered. "I'll leave markers along the way."

Evan looked dubious. "I ain't the best tracker."

"You won't miss them," Ki assured him. "They're little piles of stones. Just follow from one to the next."

"All right . . ."

"They'll be man-made and very obvious. You won't have trouble."

"I'll trust you're right." Evan was sounding more convinced.

"Don't trust me. The Indians have been doing it for years. They read those stones like trail markers."

"I ain't no Indian, but I'll manage," Evan said with a smile.

• • •

It wasn't difficult following Buck. He had, indeed, rounded up the bandits' horses, and a trail of at least a half-dozen horses was hard to miss.

The problem was not finding Buck, but rather getting to Jessie in time. Was it likely that Buck would keep Jessie in tow mile after mile, or would he, when he felt he had put enough distance between himself and the depot, use her and then discard her?

Ki did not know enough of the man to say. There was something to be argued for both sides. After his initial assault on Jessie he might lose interest in her and leave her. Whether he would leave her dead or alive was another question. But then he might keep Jessie along for his repeated pleasure. There was no reason not to. He would make better time by himself, but since he didn't expect pursuit that mattered little. Then again if he did expect to run into trouble Jessie would be his insurance.

Ki couldn't second-guess the man; he did, however, pick up his pace.

It was a hot, almost airless day, and what breeze there was blew warm on Jessie's face. The sky was a cloudless azure blue, and the strong sun beat down ceaselessly. They had been traveling west, but now as they approached a ridge of limestone outcroppings they started to make their way south. The ground underfoot became sandy and the bunch grass became sparser. Tall yuccas and thistly agaves sprang up more often, replacing the lower shrubs and tarbushes. It was a harsher terrain, though it was no less beautiful. Jessie, though, was not thinking about topography; she had more on her mind. She had been watching their route with interest, and it became obvious that Buck not only knew the lay of the land but knew where he was heading as well.

The day had elapsed in silence. Jessie was thankful that

after the first few minutes of childish boasting and bragging, Buck had quieted down.

She appreciated the peace, but more importantly, the lack of conversation meant that Buck would no longer be turning around every few seconds. That gave her hope.

Jessie was slowly working on her bonds. Not wanting to take a chance, Yvette had tied her hands tightly, but Ki had taught Jessie many things, among them a working knowledge of *hoju-jutsu*. She wasn't as skillful as Ki, but she had known enough to spread her wrists wide as her hands were being tied. Now as she rolled and squeezed them together there was some slack in the rope.

Mile after mile she worked on the bindings. Her wrists were being rubbed raw, and her chafed skin started to bleed. She ignored the pain and continued. Sore, bleeding wrists were the least of her worries.

Periodically she bent forward and pulled at the rope with her teeth. That maneuver helped greatly, but she knew it was a big risk. Buck might turn around at any moment, and if he caught her doing that all her time and effort would be wasted. The closer she got to freeing her hands the more she worried about being caught. Finally she stopped using her teeth altogether; it just wasn't worth the risk of discovery. She had been making good progress and would be free soon.

Suddenly Buck turned around. "Just want you to know this ain't nothin' personal," he said out of nowhere.

Jessie mumbled something in reply, greatly relieved that she had given up pulling at the ropes with her teeth.

Buck continued; apparently he was in a talkative mood. "I reckon now that I got me a bankroll, I deserve the finer things in life. An' I see you as just one of those things. Now take that tramp Yvette. She ain't a bad filly, but a man can have the likes of her in any fair-sized town. But you, yer refined, real re-fine-ed." He stretched out the last word into many syllables.

"You've become quite talkative," Jessie noted dryly.

"Well I didn't have much to say to them sorry lot of sodbusters back there," he answered. "And I didn't want to tip my hand till I knew what the stakes were."

"But now?"

"Well, I ain't got to be so secretive. And since we're facing a lot of miles together, I don't mind a friendly word now and then," he said with a smile. "S'long as I know you ain't one of them chatty female types. An' I think you've already proven you ain't."

Jessie mulled over his comment. That they were, according to him, facing many miles together had both its good and bad points. She started to consider the ramifications of that statement, then stopped. Her first goal was to free her hands; after that she would see.

Buck accepted her silence easily and ended the conversation. Apparently a few words at a time was his limit. Jessie didn't mind; she went back to her ropes.

But a few minutes later he stopped in a stand of honey mesquite. "Reckon it's time for a break. We've come far enough anyhow." He slid off his horse and walked over to Jessie.

Her heart sunk. She was almost free. Another few minutes and she would have made it. Worse than that, Buck would now know she had been trying to escape all morning and afternoon. For a moment she thought about spurring her horse forward in a wild bolt for freedom. But she dropped the idea. Buck was a cold, uncaring killer. If he thought she had a chance of escaping he wouldn't hesitate to put a bullet in her back. She wouldn't get more than five yards. There would be other, better opportunities. She would just have to wait—no matter what the consequence.

• • •

It didn't take but two seconds for Buck to realize what Jessie had been up to.

"You bitch," he roared, and he slapped her in the face.

Though his blow stung and nearly knocked her from the horse, Jessie didn't utter a sound.

"I'll teach you," he said as he pulled a knife from his belt. There was little Jessie could do.

He grabbed her wrist and held it tight while he cut through her bonds, then he yanked her off the horse. He dragged her to the ground then pushed the point of his blade up against her throat.

"Don't move," he hissed. "I'd hate to slip."

With his other hand he tugged roughly at Jessie's pants.

"I think I could do that easier than you." She wasn't trying to be seductive, she was worried about the knife. With the point pressing into her skin the slightest jerk could cause a cut. With Buck struggling to get her tight jeans off it only seemed a matter of time before the blade or her body slipped.

But the reasons that motivated Jessie were of little importance to Buck. He liked the idea at once. "It might be a whole lot more enjoyable, at that," he answered.

Buck removed the knife from her throat and stood up. As Jessie undid her pants she realized that her offer, an act of compliance, had put Buck off his guard. That at least was her only advantage.

Buck had worked fast. His pants were completely undone and his hard, deep-pink organ was standing straight out by the time Jessie had her pants down to her knees.

He dropped to his knees and lowered his body when Jessie struck. She was determined not to go down easy, and she gave it her best shot, bringing her knee up hard into his groin.

Buck let out a loud cry and tumbled forward. He doubled over in agony and rolled to his side, his face a deep purple.

Jessie got up quickly, but she was hampered by the pants that were wrapped around her legs. She started to run to her horse, but on her second step, a hand grabbed her ankle.

Buck yanked her leg. Jessie hit the ground hard, then blacked out.

★

Chapter 15

A sharp pain brought her around. At first it wasn't specific, just a stabbing somewhere in her head, but then it became much more real and immediate. She tasted a warm, sticky liquid in her mouth—blood, her own. And the ringing in her ears. And the pain in her right side.

Then her eyes focused, and she saw Buck standing over her. He was yelling. Slowly the words came to her; vile, ugly, single syllables. And his hand kept coming down and hitting her in the face. Her head was throbbing, but the side of her face was numb. She could feel the blow land, but she didn't feel the pain on impact. That would come later.

Jessie raised her hands to protect her face. Her mind was clearing quickly. She considered trying another kick, when Buck mysteriously stopped and backed off.

Then, struggling to get up, Jessie saw why. Buck was pulling up his pants. His once erect manhood now lay there limp and flaccid; his seed, a thick, white cream, spread dripping down his thigh.

Jessie knew this was her chance, but her beaten and bruised body would not react.

His passion spent, Buck dragged her to her feet and threw her into the saddle. Her hands were again tied and then they were on their way.

Her mind was now clear, and it brought to her a full realization of the pain. She concentrated on ways to escape, but after a while she relaxed and closed her eyes. Soon she slumped forward, exhausted and hurting.

The sun had set, and the sky was a light gray. It was still another hour before nightfall. It had been a long day in the saddle, and Jessie was glad when they finally stopped for the night. It felt good to stretch out her sore body on the ground.

Buck went about preparing dinner. Not a word had passed between them. Jessie didn't think he regretted the beating as much as he did his poor sign of virility.

When he handed her a plate of beans she spoke up. "You're making a big mistake," she began.

"How do you figure?" he asked, seemingly eager to converse.

"I'm a wealthy woman," she replied. "I own, among other things, a large Texas ranch. There are those who'll pay a lot of money to make sure I return unharmed."

Buck was thinking it over. Apparently the strength of his greed was not to be underestimated.

"I'll overlook today's incident as an unfortunate mistake. As long as you don't lay another hand on me."

Buck laughed. "A man could always use some more money. But right now I'm fixed just fine. What I need now ain't money." His insinuation was clear.

"You touch me and the deal's off," Jessie said firmly.

"Seems to me if they'll pay money to have you returned unharmed, they'd be just as happy to have you returned alive."

Jessie shook her head.

Buck continued. "And you did say 'unharmed.' What I plan on doing ain't what you'd call harm, least not to the likes of you." He let out a mean laugh. "I reckon you might even enjoy it some."

Jessie tried and lost. Bribery would not work. There were other ways. "You'll have to do a whole lot better than this afternoon," she said spitefully.

Buck turned red.

Jessie hoped she could anger him into making a foolish mistake. She needed him again. "I've seen jackrabbits last longer," she said with a nasty chuckle of her own.

"You ain't going to be laughing when I get through with you," Buck swore.

"And how long will that be, five seconds?"

Buck threw his plate down and stood up.

Just then a stranger walked into the camp. Both Jessie and Buck had been so intent in their discussion they did not hear his approach.

"Evenin'," the stranger said. "Saw the light of yer fire."

"Beat it," Buck growled suspiciously.

"That ain't no way to show hospitality," the stranger said. His slow smile exposed a row of crooked, stained teeth.

"We don't want no company. Get on yer way."

"Can't do that," the stranger said.

"You'd best," Buck warned.

"Not till I get what I came for. But I'm willin' to trade."

"I ain't going to tell you again," Buck said as he dropped his gun hand down to his side.

The stranger remained firm. "You got somethin' I want, but I got somethin' you want, too. . . ."

165

"And what's that, old man?" Buck asked scornfully.

"Yer life."

Late in the day Ki found the wash where Buck and Jessie had stopped. It appeared to be only a short rest; there was no trace of a cookfire. Ki did find some unusual marks in the dirt, though. With iron-clad fortitude he didn't dwell on what they might represent, and pushed on.

But subconsciously those marks were having their effect. The dirt clearly showed signs of a struggle. There were also two spots where a body had lain prone. It was nothing conclusive, but Ki began to wonder if he was already too late.

In answer to that question he broke into a run. He was even more determined to get to Jessie, and quickly.

As the situation grew bleak Ki found his resolve strengthening. He wasn't going to let her remain in that killer's hands any longer than necessary. That he had to travel by foot while they rode was no longer a valid excuse. There was no good excuse whatsoever. He wasn't going to let Jessie down, even if he had to run the whole way.

But, as Ki had often experienced in the past, when the human spirit fought against unusual odds, fate often intervened to balance the contest.

A quarter of a mile away Ki found the bandit's horses grazing on sparse fluffgrass. Apparently Buck had no longer felt the need to drive the horses any farther. They were already a considerable distance away from the depot, and it was unlikely that someone would track them this far on foot. The only other reason to take the horses would be for their monetary value, but Buck already had enough of that.

Ki approached the fastest-looking horse. He moved slowly, not wanting to scare away the animal. If every time

Ki reached for him the horse bolted it could take hours to catch the animal. And hours was what Ki did not have. He was trying to make up time, not lose it.

But he had no difficulty. Partially because of his skill in dealing with animals and also in part because it seemed the horse remembered him from their earlier encounter.

Once mounted, he gathered up the other horses and pointed them in the direction of the depot.

Then Ki urged his horse into a full-speed run. He wasn't as graceful riding bareback as Jessie; he didn't move as fluidly. But right now he wasn't concerned with form. He pressed his legs hard against the animal's sides, bouncing along as he pushed the horse to its limit.

He continued long into the night. Though it was much slower going, he was able to track by the light of the moon. But when the trail turned south he became a little worried. A low ridge had sprung up in the distance, and Ki wondered if Buck would eventually cut in for the higher ground. Ki didn't want to miss that turn and then have to waste precious hours backtracking.

Ki moved slower, checking for signs much more frequently. As he did so, he never forgot to leave his stone markers for Evan.

Finally, in the early hours of the morning, Ki stopped. For the sake of the horse, he had been resting periodically, but they were short stops. Now he figured it was best to let the horse get some sleep. It wasn't a bad idea for himself, either. When he faced Buck he wanted to be sharp and alert.

Though Ki knew he couldn't really formulate a plan of action until he had actually caught up with Buck, his mind was already beginning to work on the possibilities. Foremost was the necessity of getting Jessie away from Buck.

At the time, Ki didn't realize how easily that would be

accomplished. He also didn't realize that Buck was now the least of his concerns.

It happened so quickly, Jessie wasn't sure she saw it correctly.

Buck reached for his gun. It wasn't a lightning-fast draw. Perhaps he didn't feel threatened by the stranger, perhaps he never intended to use the weapon as anything more than an encouragement to induce the stranger to move on his way.

The stranger stood there, watching Buck closely. Jessie never saw him move. True, she, too, was watching Buck, but her line of sight also took in the stranger. And she would swear he hardly moved. Though whether or not he did was a moot point.

There was a loud boom; a flash of blue and orange fire, and then the acrid smell of black powder.

It took only a fraction of a second. But in that time Buck's brains and blood and flesh were scattered far, as his life was blown from his body.

The stranger had walked in carrying what looked like a bedroll. Jessie had thought nothing of it. Apparently neither had Buck. It was a fatal mistake.

He carried the roll lengthwise, gripping it from behind. It hung down vertically, parallel to his leg. Only now did Jessie realize that the blanket concealed a shotgun. All the stranger had to do was tilt his wrist to bring the scattergun to bear on Buck. His finger was no doubt already on the trigger. Buck hadn't stood a chance.

"Gets them every time," the stranger said, with practiced calm.

Jessie was too stunned to answer.

"No need to thank me," the man continued. "Fact is, Miss Starbuck, when all is said and done, *thanks* won't be the right word."

Jessie was even more surprised that he knew her name —indeed, so surprised that she missed the innuendo in his words. "I don't believe we've had the pleasure of meeting. But I do consider it a pleasure."

"I wouldn't," he said flatly.

For the first time Jessie saw the aura of evil that surrounded the man. He seemed bathed in hate, and his eyes, though tired, were alive and crackling with black intent.

"I don't understand," she said honestly.

"You will, Miss Starbuck. Very shortly it will all become painfully clear."

Jessie looked confused. "I'm afraid I don't understand," she repeated. "My name's Yvette. Yvette DeVeau. I'm from Little Springs. And though I'm mighty glad you rescued me from the likes of him, I can't rightly say that I'm the person you were hoping for."

For a second she thought she had him going, but then he broke into a hearty laugh. "If I didn't know that you were as shrewd as your father, I might have believed you."

Though it obviously wasn't working, Jessie kept up the charade. She felt it was her only hope. "My father hails from Saint Joe and didn't account for much more than our five-acre farm."

"Then why is an Oriental bodyguard hot on your trail? Ki, I believe he is called."

Jessie couldn't hide her look of hope.

The stranger smiled. "He is just a few miles back, Miss Starbuck—or should I call you Jessica?"

"I don't know why you keep thinking that—" Jessie protested.

"Because I'm no fool," the stranger snapped. Then he brought his temper under control. "You may carry on this game if you wish; it's no matter to me."

"It's no game," Jessie said sincerely.

"No, it isn't," the stranger agreed.

"So if you keep thinking I'm this Jessica Star—whatever . . ."

The stranger smiled. "You are a lot like your father, in looks and in spirit. He would also play a hand out to the very end. And he never admitted defeat, either. Not even at the very end. Why, I imagine he died kicking. . . ."

"What do you know about my father's death?" she said quickly, her eyes ablaze. "My father was murdered."

"I know. I cried when I heard." He saw the look in her eyes soften and he laughed. "But don't mistake me for a friend. Hardly. I cried because I wanted to be there to watch him die."

Jessie started to get up, but her body moved slowly.

"Stay where you are," he ordered. "I've got another load in the other barrel." He didn't even bother showing her the gun. She lay back down.

"I suggest you try and get some sleep," he continued. "We have some more riding to do tomorrow, and I want you at your best."

Jessie didn't argue. She did need some rest, but more importantly the sooner they went to sleep, the sooner she had a chance at escape. Her new captor made no effort to tie her.

The stranger, though, must have been reading her mind. "I wouldn't think about sneaking off. You see, I don't sleep at night," he informed her. "And I especially won't be sleeping tonight."

Jessie turned and faced the other way.

"And just in case you're willing to test me, I should warn you that I won't hesitate to empty this gun into your back. Although it would ruin my plans. . . ."

"I wouldn't think of ruining your plans," Jessie said, then closed her eyes.

• • •

The sun was already shining when Jessie awoke. The night's sleep had done her good. She was feeling sore, and her bruises were still sensitive, but her head was clear and her body's reaction time and responses were near normal.

She also felt better mentally. Though her new captor was clearly as deadly as Buck and her situation had not really improved any, she felt much better knowing Ki wasn't far behind.

When she turned over, the stranger, as promised, sat watching her. "Throw me your bandana," he said.

She took it from around her neck and threw it to him.

He grabbed it and dropped it next to Buck's body. Then he picked up a small burlap bag, untied a string at the top, and placed it under the bandana. Slowly he pulled the bag away. He offered no explanation.

"Now get up on that horse, and remember, this greener is going to be following you the whole way."

Jessie didn't need to be reminded about the shotgun. Buck's barely recognizable body, still where it had dropped, was more than enough to stifle any idea Jessie had for a quick getaway.

"What was that in the bag?" she asked as they started off.

"That's a little surprise for your would-be hero," he said, then he told her.

Jessie went pale.

Chapter 16

From what was left of his face there was no way to tell who the man was. But Ki had no doubts. If nothing else, he recognized the clothes.

Then he spotted the bandana lying on the ground. He thought it was Jessie's but he couldn't be sure; one looked much like another. He would know by smelling it. Perhaps there was even a message of some sort under it.

He bent down to pick it up.

He had barely lifted the red cloth, when he felt it.

Sharp, daggerlike pincers, then a painful, stinging barb.

Automatically his left hand swatted at his wrist. The small brown spider fell away, dead; but it was too late. The scorpion had already stung.

There were over a hundred different species of scorpion. Though most were poisonous, only a few proved fatal to man.

Carefully—where there was one scorpion there could be more—Ki kneeled and studied the dead spider. It was only about two and a half inches long, tan, with a faint yellow-green stripe. Ki didn't know enough to identify the species, but he had a bad feeling about it. He did know that the larger scorpions, fairly common in the deserts of Texas, were not fatal. These smaller ones he wasn't sure of. And that uncertainty had him worried.

The sudden pain in his wrist, a sign of potent venom, also had him worried.

He ripped off the sleeve of his shirt, took Carl's knife from his pocket, and fashioned a tourniquet on his forearm.

Ki knew the best thing to do, this far away from town and a doctor, was to remain passive and immobile. But that was out of the question.

He picked up Buck's revolver. Then, out of habit, he cracked open the cylinder to check the load. The gun was empty. Then Ki saw that the man's cartridge belt was also empty.

Someone had deliberately taken the bullets but had left the gun. Another man, someone less thorough than Ki, might have just pocketed the weapon and never realized that it was empty—until it was too late.

With sudden insight Ki wondered if the scorpion had also been placed there deliberately. Ki would almost certainly have picked up the bandana. It was hard to miss the red cloth. And scorpions were nocturnal creatures. During the heat of the day they would wait moitionless under a stone, bark, or in this case, a bandana.

Ki didn't like the implications. But there was nothing he could do but get to Jessie as fast as possible.

Was this day hotter than the others? Then why, Ki wondered, was he sweating so profusely? The swelling in his hand was the first bad sign. The headache and nausea that soon followed only confirmed his suspicions.

The bite was poisonous; now it only remained to see

how deadly the venom was. A few hours of pain and sickness were only a minor discomfort. But anything more serious . . . Anything more serious and what would happen to Jessie?

Ki didn't like the answer. It was a race against time. He pushed his horse faster.

Luckily, the trail was easy to read. For a moment Ki even worried that it was too easy. Was he being lured into a trap? He couldn't help but think of the fly and the waiting spider. Something inside his feverish head made him laugh at the thought. He may have been stung once, but he was no defenseless fly. He had a bite of his own.

Jessie found out little more about the stranger or his mission. Conversation was difficult. He made her ride in front, leading the way, while he rode a few feet behind, periodically issuing a few directions.

Jessie didn't have to turn around to know the shotgun was pointed right at her back. She kept her eyes forward, and her mouth shut, waiting for her captor to speak first. He never did.

They were heading straight for the low mountain ridge. That didn't surprise Jessie, as mountains were a good place to lose a trail. However, she was surprised that once they hit the foothills, they veered to the north, following a dry river bed.

An hour up the gulch, they stopped in front of an abandoned mine shaft.

"This is it," the stranger announced. "The Starbuck burial grounds."

He took her deep into the mine shaft, and tied her to one of the upright beams.

"Hear that scratchin'? Those are rats. Probably a few

175

rattlers in here too, but you won't hear those," the stranger said. "In a while, when your eyes get accustomed to the dark, then you'll start seeing the little creatures as they crawl around. And pretty soon, once they find out you can't harm them, you'll feel them crawling up your legs, picking at your skin for crumbs. And if you start getting impatient, I have some molasses in my pack. Some on your face sure will speed up the process. But with or without it, they'll soon be licking the saliva off of your lips."

"Why are you doing this?" Jessie asked. Her voice was calm, but she had to struggle to keep it that way.

"Just thought I'd let you know what you're in for."

"But why?" she repeated.

"Just thought I'd give you the benefit of my experience," he answered. "You see, I know all about dark holes and rats, and spiders."

"I don't even know who you are."

He ignored her and went on, suddenly very talkative. "You think it will help if you don't go to sleep. I didn't go to sleep myself for days."

"What are you talking about?" Jessie almost shouted. The ravings of this lunatic were almost more frightening than the prospects of rats and snakes crawling all over her. Almost.

"Still can't sleep at nights. But it don't help much, staying awake, Miss Starbuck. All it does is let you see the little critters, see them real close. But I don't suppose you'll heed my advice. You'll stay up just like I did, just like everyone does. You'll get used to sleeping in the day, when your friends don't come out crawling." He let out a shrill laugh. "Problem is, down here, when is it day? Where's the sun? When do those creatures sleep? You won't know, Miss Starbuck; you just won't know."

"Who are you?" Jessie asked again. "And why are you doing this to me?"

176

"I'm a man who knows all about dark holes filled with rats."

Jessie thought about his pockmarked complexion. She had naturally assumed it was due to a bout with the pox, but now she shuddered at the thought of rats picking at his face, leaving tiny blood-dripping holes.

"And why am I doing this to you?" he continued. "Because I can't do it to your father."

He got up and headed out. "Time to set a fire for Ki. I wouldn't want him to miss us."

"He'll kill you," Jessie snapped.

The stranger laughed. "He'll certain try, but I doubt he'll be in any condition to kill anything."

"What even makes you think the scorpion will have bitten him?" Jessie asked, though she knew it was a foolish question.

"I know all about spiders."

"He'll at least be able to free me," she countered.

"I do hope so. You see, Miss Starbuck, that's not just wire holding you to that point, it's a tripwire connected to a detonator, which in turn connects to packs of TNT. . . . You'll be trapped in here. With the rats. They won't mind. You'll die a slow, miserable death."

When he returned a few minutes later Jessie had another question. "You went to a lot of trouble to set this up," she began. "It's all so well planned."

"Years, Miss Starbuck. It took years with nothing else to do but plan."

"But how did you know we'd be by this way?"

The stranger laughed. "I sent you that message about the Mora."

"You!"

He nodded. "Everything was well thought out, every

177

step, every detail. But I had plenty of time to get it right," he added sharply.

"But why?" she asked again, though now she thought she understood.

"Your father sent me to prison. I owe him this." He spoke the words slowly, deliberately. They were full of hate.

"Who are you?"

The stranger laughed. "I lost my name in the Federal penitentary—in a dark, dank hole filled with rats." Jessie started to speak but he continued. "Though I think you'll find my name somewhere in that black book of your father's. . . ."

"The log book he kept of his enemies?"

"Appropriately put."

"What's your name?" Jessie demanded to know.

"Does it matter?" There was a moment's pause before his voice filled the darkness. "Call me Death."

Ki saw the fire flickering in the distance. He turned his horse towards it, then slumped forward over the animal.

His eyes were burning, his head was light, and he was still dizzy, but the nausea had passed. He knew he was far from his best physically, but he struggled to clear his head. He would have to rely on his wits to get Jessie out of this one.

Ki wondered about the fire. Was it simply carelessness, or did Jessie's captor think Ki was already in a state of delirium, withering somewhere in the dirt? Ki ruled out the first choice immediately. The man had killed Buck, taken Jessie, and sprung a surprise on Ki. It didn't sound like the work of a careless individual.

Ki couldn't cut through the fog in his brain. He couldn't figure out the reason. It made no sense. But that in itself caused him to proceed with caution. He went on instinct;

and like an animal approaching the unknown, Ki suspected a trap.

He stopped, dismounted, and gathered up a few stones. He couldn't remember why he did it, he just knew it was something he had been doing, something he had to do, something he would continue to do.

He got back up on his horse, and started the animal towards the light of the distant fire, never realizing that the flames were indeed a beacon, a guiding light leading him straight to doom.

Ki, outlined against the fire behind him, stood in the mouth of the tunnel. The flames cast their light a few yards into the mine; then darkness took over. He ventured forth slowly, listening, letting his eyes grow accustomed to the dark. An observer would have easily mistaken his caution for physical weakness.

The tunnel branched off and Ki stood at the fork.

"Ki, it's a trap," Jessie shouted.

Her voice was like an bullwhip snapping his brain awake.

"Go back, Ki," she called again.

"Jessie . . ." he answered and rushed forward, tripping as he did so.

A shrill laugh echoed off the rock walls. "There's your shining knight to the rescue," a voice said derisively. "He can barely walk."

"I'll kill you, you bastard," Ki said standing, but a moment later he fell back down to his knees.

Jessie was confused. Ki never used profane language. Did he do so now as a signal to Jessie, or was it an indication of what the scorpion's venom had done to him?

"I'll save you, Jessie," Ki promised, as he staggered like a drunk.

"No, there are explosives wired to me," she warned.

"I'll kill him," Ki bellowed. "Where are you, you damn slime. Show your face." Ki lunged forward and fell on his face.

. The stranger laughed again, and Ki began to crawl towards the voice.

"Crawl, Ki. Crawl to me," he cackled.

"I'll rip you apart, I'll kill you. . . ."

Years of imprisonment, of anger, hatred, and frustration came forth in the stranger's near hysterical howls.

"I swear on my father's ancestors, you'll die at my hands," Ki shrieked back.

Jessie was no longer worried. She had ultimate faith in Ki.

While Ki's body was inching forward his mind was racing ahead. His fuzzy thoughts had cleared instantly upon hearing Jessie, but his body was still suspect. He didn't know how well he would be able to counteract the effects of the scorpion's poison. In fact he wouldn't know till he put himself to the test. And until that moment he wanted to give himself every advantage possible.

The first being the element of surprise, or, more specifically, the element of deceit. The stranger naturally assumed that Ki was weak and confused. Ki saw no reason to change the man's mind, and even played it up.

Ki had another very real advantage. His eyes, which had been burning and tearing for hours, were of no use in the dark mine. It was actually a relief not to have to rely on them. His hearing, though, once his head cleared, seemed to be functioning perfectly. Every laugh of the stranger's, every sound, allowed Ki to move towards the man's position.

Then Ki realized what was perhaps his best advantage. "Keep laughing, you fool, and I'll put a bullet right between your eyes," he shouted confidently.

The spontaneous shriek that the man emitted told Ki two

things. One, his hunch was right, and two, he was very close.

Ki undid the tourniquet on his forearm and removed the knife that held it tight.

"Shoot me, Ki. Stand up and shoot me," the stranger urged crazily.

The man was no doubt shrewd and cunning. He would know that Ki did not use firearms. Therefore the gun Ki threatened to use had to be Buck's more than useless weapon. That was why the stranger thought it all so funny. That offered Ki hope.

Ki held the knife in his left hand. He was almost as capable with his left hand as with his right. But that "almost" bothered him. He would only have one chance. He would have to get close.

"Jessie, Jessie, I can't see," he cried as he struggled to his feet, and staggered around in a circle.

"This way, Ki. I'm over here," the stranger called out.

Ki turned and pitched forward. His left hand flung in front of him.

"Come get meee . . ." The words trailed off into a surprised gasp.

The hunting knife had found its mark.

Ki heard the body drop. Then there was a large explosion behind him. *"Jessie?!"*

"I'm all right," she called back.

Ki grew suddenly weak, and crumpled to the floor.

"Ki?" There was no answer. She began to tug at her bonds. There was no reason not to. The explosives had already gone off, she could do no more damage by pulling at the tripwire that held her.

She was soon free; the wire had not been tied too tightly, and a few hard snaps gave her a lot of play.

Feeling around, she eventually found Ki. Though he

181

was unconscious he seemed unhurt; there was no bleeding and no debris had fallen on him. He was, though, extremely hot to the touch. She placed him down gently, and went in search of her captor.

She found him a moment later, dead, slumped over the detonator.

A quick search of his pockets found a few matches. She struck one on the wall. Little things everywhere scurried into cracks and behind rocks. She gave an involuntary shudder.

Another match later she had assessed their situation, and it wasn't good.

Not all the dynamite had exploded. Apparently the rats, which the stranger had been so keen on, had clawed and gnawed through some of the wires. But one pack, over by the entrance, did detonate. And now they were trapped.

Trapped with no food, no water, and the scurrying of hungry rodents.

Jessie didn't know how long she sat there with Ki's head in her lap. She suspected it was at least twelve hours. Twelve hours of throwing stones and making noises to keep the curious things at bay. She thought about trying to light a small fire, but decided against it. Jessie didn't know how much air they had in the tunnel, and she didn't want to waste any of it by burning it up.

But then her long vigil ended. Ki stirred and sat up.

"Mornin' " Jessie said smiling. "Least I think it is. How do you feel?"

"Fine," he answered.

"You had me worried."

"I'm sorry, Jessie. I had to act that way to put him off his guard."

"Not that. I knew what you were doing. That line about your father's ancestors was the tip."

"I'd had hoped you'd get it."

"I did. Your mother's Oriental family would have been a normal reference, but you wouldn't think of your American lineage as 'ancestors.'"

Ki nodded. "Then why were you worried?"

"You were burning up, and blacked out for some time."

"A scorpion sting . . ."

"I know," Jessie answered. "I think a man less strong than yourself might have died."

"That still might be a possibility," Ki began.

"I thought you said you feel fine." Jessie said quickly.

"One can feel fine, and still die of thirst, starvation, or suffocation."

Jessie understood.

"We still have to get out of here," Ki said as he got up, and went to the pile of rock that blocked their exit.

Just then he heard a scraping sound. "Did you hear that?" he asked.

"Rats," Jessie answered.

"No, listen." Then they both heard it.

To end any of their doubts they finally heard Evan's voice. "Ki? Jessie?"

A few hours later the first whiff of fresh air entered the tunnel. A crack of light followed shortly after.

Ki and Jessie worked on their side, while Evan, Blain, and Yvette worked from the outside.

A finger clawed its way through the mound of rock and earth. Jessie and Ki eagerly reached out for it.

At that moment they both shared the very same thought. Jessie and Ki exchanged looks, but neither of them spoke. How fitting that these one-time strangers, folks which they chose to befriend and aid, had now arrived to save their own lives.

Watch for

LONE STAR AND THE SILVER BANDITS

seventy-second novel in the exciting
LONE STAR
series from Jove

coming in August!